Over the years I've invented all these come-backs to what girls might say if I tried anything with them. I was sure Leslie would say something like "Who the hell do you think you are?" or "Cut it out, you jerk!" But she just lay back, put her arms around my neck, and kissed me. I figured: *Well, at some point she'll say stop,* but she didn't. She even helped me! When I put my hand down in her jeans, she kind of wriggled them off, and as soon as that happened, she took off her T-shirt. To make a long story short, we actually ended up doing it. . . .

Fawcett Juniper Books
by Norma Klein:

ANGEL FACE

BEGINNERS' LOVE

BIZOU

FAMILY SECRETS

GIVE AND TAKE

IT'S OK IF YOU DON'T LOVE ME

LOVE IS ONE OF THE CHOICES

THE QUEEN OF THE WHAT IFS

SNAPSHOTS

FAMILY SECRETS

Norma Klein

FAWCETT JUNIPER • NEW YORK

FOR AMY EHRLICH

RLI: $\frac{\text{VL: 5 + up}}{\text{IL: 9 + up}}$

A Fawcett Juniper Book
Published by Ballantine Books

Library of Congress Catalog Card Number: 85-6997

ISBN 0-449-70195-6

This edition published by arrangement with Dial Books, a division of E. P. Dutton

Manufactured in the United States of America

First Ballantine Books Edition: March 1987

PART I

Something I Never Told You

LESLIE PULLED HER SHIRT BACK OVER HER HEAD, SHAKING the sand out. I still feel funny seeing her naked. I looked out at the ocean till she had it back on.

Leslie and I are still awkward together. Though we've known each other all our lives, we've only been lovers for a month. During the year, she lives in Manhattan with her family, and I live in Westport with mine. But every summer since we were babies both our families have come to Fire Island, where we have beach houses in the same area. As kids we always horsed around, went sailing or sometimes played chess or tennis. If there was a party, my mother would say, "Why don't you take Leslie?" and sometimes I would. But it was nothing especially romantic. I'm not what you'd call one of the world's great lovers, to put it mildly. Till last month my experience with girls was pretty sparse. I'd certainly thought about them a lot, but nothing ever got off the ground, as it were.

The couple of times a girl seemed to like me, even a little, I felt like I could tell, but with Leslie I never got that feeling. I always assumed she did things with me partly because her mother said, "How about going with Peter? He's a nice boy." So I was really surprised when she came over to me last month at a party and asked if I felt like taking a walk with her on the beach. I'd been just standing around, not doing much, wondering if I should go home. "Sure," I said. "I haven't got anything better to do." Which in retrospect wasn't the warmest response, especially given what followed.

We ended up sitting in a cove down at the end of the beach. It was a cloudy, soft, beautiful night. I can't even remember exactly what started it. I think I leaned over for some reason, and about one second later we were kissing. Over the years I've invented all these comebacks to what girls might say if I tried anything with them. I was sure Leslie would say something like "Who the hell do you think you are?" or "Cut it out, you jerk!" But she just lay back, put her arms around my neck, and kissed me. I figured: *Well, at some point she'll say stop,* but she didn't. She even helped me! When I put my hand down in her jeans, she kind of wriggled them off, and as soon as that happened, she took off her T-shirt. To make a long story short, we actually ended up doing it.

I thought for sure she'd be mad afterward. I figured maybe she'd gotten slightly stoned at the party and would come to with a horrible shock. But she just lay there, looking at me contemplatively, not saying much, but not seeming angry either. It was strange. We were the same people we'd been a couple hours earlier, but everything seemed completely different. I remember a teacher in Sex Ed telling us, "Sex is an intensifier. It makes whatever you already feel that much stronger." Before that night Leslie had been a fairly nice girl whom I felt more at ease with than most. Now suddenly it seemed like she had some kind of frightening power over me. If she'd said anything critical right then, I would have been totally demolished. But she just sat up, kissed me, and said, "They say first times are so awful. Actually I thought that was kind of nice. Didn't you?"

I think she knew I did. We got it established that it was the first time for both of us, with anyone. Neither of us had ever done much of anything with the opposite sex. In short we were real neophytes. I'm glad. A girl with lots of experience would have scared me shitless. Then came the *really* hard part. It's one thing to conveniently and painlessly lose your virginity with a girl you've known since you were in diapers, but what then? After a string of horribly awkward pauses, we managed to let each other know that as long as we had survived the first time, we might as well take it from there. Which we have done. Not every day, but a few times a week. Oh, hell, exactly ten times. I'm not blasé enough yet to lose count. In fact, each time is being stored in my mind like some video cassette that I can play in my head during senior year.

"There's something I never told you," Leslie said. She looked out at the ocean which was about twenty feet away.

"What?" I asked. I try not to ogle Leslie afterward, but she looks incredibly pretty with her short black hair ruffled and her face slightly pink and flushed.

"I was looking for some Kotex yesterday, and I found my mother's diary."

"Yeah?"

Leslie frowned. "I read it."

"So, what'd you find out? Anything interesting?" Leslie's mother is a redhead, very sports minded, with a terrific figure, much more the bouncy, cheerleader type than Leslie is, even if she's got to be forty or thereabouts.

Leslie was poking at the ground with a stick. "It's something terrible."

"What?" For some reason her grimness made me want to laugh, maybe out of nervousness.

She looked straight at me with her big, intense brown eyes. "She's making it with your father."

"You're kidding."

"Sure, I'm kidding. Big joke."

"Jesus." Actually, the fact that my father isn't faithful to my mother is something I've been aware of for some time now. They've had some fairly hair-raising fights over the last few years, especially since my two older brothers, Cliff and Ken, went off to college. My father's very handsome—he makes his living at it, in fact. He does commercials for TV. Women flirt with him, and he flirts with them. Whereas my mother is a little on the plump side, like me, gray haired, and more what you'd call the homebody type.

"What should we do about it?" Leslie asked.

"Nothing. How can we do anything? You don't want her to know you read her private papers, do you?"

"Do you think it'll just blow over?"

"Les, how can I know? Has it been going on long?"

"A year and a half! They're in love! Peter, listen, I really think this is serious. I got the feeling they were not, you should pardon the expression, just fucking around."

"Maybe your mother isn't."

"But you think your father is? She claims he's talked about leaving your mother. They've even looked at co-ops together. In fact— Oh, my God . . . Didn't you say before your father was in the city on a job for a couple of days?"

"Sure. So?"

"Guess where Mom is?" Leslie let out a moan. "Peter, they're looking at apartments! They're probably right this *second* buying an eight-room co-op apartment!"

"Les, come on." I reached out and pulled her over next to me.

"You think I'm jumping the gun? You think I'm imagining things? Tell me what you think."

I cleared my throat. "Okay, here's what I think. I think, yes, they are having an affair, and maybe your mother's in love, and maybe my father has said he's in love and made various promises, but no, I don't think he'll end up leaving my mom and marrying yours."

"Why not?"

"He's been doing this kind of thing for years. He wants a little action on the side, not a new wife."

Leslie sighed. "God, you're cynical. Really? How do you know that's what he wants?"

"I live with him, he's my father. He's a totally self-centered bastard."

Leslie looked at me, frowning. "You really hate him, don't you?"

"No, I don't hate him. But he treats my mother like shit, he thinks I'm a total loser, he's always bugging me about my weight—"

"Yeah, I've noticed that," Leslie said. She was silent a moment. "Poor Daddy."

Leslie's father is a short, portly neurologist who loves baroque music and talks in a jocular, ironical way most of the time. I could see him getting on someone's nerves. But mainly I could imagine the whole thing physically—Dad and Leslie's mother are thin, bright eyed, sexy, on the make. Yeah, I could imagine it all too well. "Maybe your father will find someone else," I said, more to say something than because I thought it was true.

"I thought you said nothing was going to happen." She looked up at me accusingly.

"He can still find someone."

"He's such a sweetie, poor old thing. Maybe if he lost

some weight. Your father's in such incredible shape! I usually don't notice men's bodies, but when we were playing doubles the other day, I looked at him and thought, *Wow!*"

I felt angry, though every word of it was true, and I'm sure Leslie's reaction is typical of most women. My father plays tennis all summer and squash all winter. He doesn't have an ounce of fat on him. It's kind of disgusting to have a father whom your girl friends think is in better shape than you are, when you're seventeen and he's forty-seven. "Maybe you ought to make a play for him," I said.

"Peter!"

"Maybe he needs a younger woman to get his mind off your mother."

Leslie sat forward. "Why do you say things like that? I don't understand you. You can be so warm and understanding and then suddenly so sarcastic and shitty."

I sighed. "I'm sorry, Les. I'm just jealous of him, I guess."

Leslie took my hand. "But you're a wonderful person. That's so much more important. Who cares about bodies?"

"I do."

We both laughed.

"I mean, I love your body too," Leslie said, blushing. "Why would we be here otherwise?"

"I thought we were just getting some outdoor exercise, getting a good tan." I love teasing Leslie.

"Peter . . . isn't my body important to you?"

"Your body," I said solemnly, "is the most important thing in my life. I think about it more than any other single topic. I dream about it."

Leslie giggled. "Do you really?"

"Absolutely. Obscene, manic, incredible dreams."

She blushed again. "I dream about you too. God, aren't we awful, both of us?"

"No, just two red-blooded American teenagers. If anything, we're probably undersexed. Seventeen and still virgins until last month. That won't get us into the *Guinness Book of World Records*."

"I guess not." Leslie leaned back in my arms again. She felt warm and sweaty and good. "You could say we're making up for lost time."

"Definitely." I thought of my brothers. Cliff is four years older than me; Ken is three years older. Cliff looks like my father, and Ken doesn't look like either of my parents; they both had girl friends in high school, and I'm sure they saw a lot more action than I ever did.

I glanced at my watch. It was noon, and I'd promised Mom I'd be back for lunch. "We'd better go."

Leslie nodded and stood up. She's a foot shorter than me and slender, with small high breasts. Her nose comes up to my nipples. We'd be a disaster trying to dance close. "Well, I'll let you know if anything develops. Keep an eye on your father when he comes home. Look for telltale signs."

"Like the contract for an eight-room co-op in his briefcase?"

"Right." She sighed. "I hate being with Daddy now, me knowing while he's such an innocent."

"Maybe he's not," I suggested.

"He is," Leslie insisted. She gave me a big hug. "See you."

I waited till she was out of sight. Then I walked back to our house to have lunch with my mother.

Other People's Secrets

ON THE WAY HOME FROM THE BEACH I STARTED THINKING about Mira. Sometimes I think it's all her fault that I got involved with Peter. You could say I'm just using her as a scapegoat, trying to find excuses, but if she hadn't come back from the Experiment in International Living after our sophomore year yapping on and on about her grand and glorious affair with this Frenchman, Jacques, maybe I wouldn't even have thought about being a virgin or not being one. We've been friends since second grade and Mira's always been the first to do everything. It's like she just has to be first. Maybe if I thought she was really better than me, I wouldn't mind, but I don't really believe that and deep down I do mind. It isn't just in acting—we're both good actresses, the best in school probably, and are always competing for the same parts. It's in all kinds of other things. Somehow I always seem to end up taking my cues from Mira. If she decides something is important, it is.

I think I was also influenced by playing Jenny in *The Prime of Miss Jean Brodie* last year. Brodie kept saying, "Jenny will be famous for sex," and even though I was only sixteen then, I would wonder if it was going to be true of me. On the basis of my looks anyone would say no. I've always looked much younger than I actually am. In acting I had an edge when it came to parts like Peter Pan or Ariel. I could have been typecast in *The Diary of Anne Frank:* big eyes, too skinny, intense. Besides, I never wanted to rush into sex with just anyone. It could have been partly cowardice. I wanted the first time to be with someone I knew really well and felt I could trust.

I've always felt more at ease with Peter than with most boys. Probably going to an all-girls school hasn't been good for me in that way. I never learned to be relaxed and joke around with boys, the way I might've if I'd gone to a coed school. Another reason boys seem so unfamiliar to me is my not having any brothers. Possibly if I had one, I'd know what to do and how to act around boys. If I had a brother, I wouldn't mind if he was like Peter. It's not just that Peter's quiet like me and what Mom calls a loner in a not very approving way. It's that, even though he's superbright and applying to Harvard for early admission, he doesn't inundate you with all his achievements the way lots of guys do. In fact, I wouldn't even have known about things like his winning the Westinghouse Science Competition if it weren't for his mother telling mine. Peter reminds me of a whale, though I'd never tell him that because he'd assume it was an insult. He's pathologically insecure about his weight. I suppose it would be better if he lost some, but to me he seems solid and round and comfortable and gentle. Maybe more like a dolphin actually since they're supposed to be so smart and also friendly once you win them over.

I have to admit, now that it's worked out, and Peter didn't cringe or scream with horror or seem to despise me after we made love, that I get such a kick out of knowing *I* seduced *him*. I look at myself in the mirror, and suddenly I look seductive and alluring. I've even been slathering on eye makeup before I go to see him, which normally I'd never do on the beach in summer. Peter says he feels I have power over him and that it makes him nervous. It makes *me* feel wonderful! I've never had power over *anyone* before, never felt powerful in any sense of the word, except maybe on stage. Before this I never even felt boys could be vulnerable, but now, when I look at Peter sometimes, especially right after we've made love, he has such a guarded but adoring expression. It makes me so happy.

In a way the happiness has been a shield against this thing about Mom and Peter's father. If I had found out last summer, I would've just gone to pieces. Now, though it hurts horribly, I remember how I feel after Peter and I make love and think: *Maybe that's why Mom is doing it*. Maybe she needed that and wasn't getting it with Daddy. I love Daddy, maybe to excess almost, but he isn't sexy in any conventional way. With me he can be warm and lovely, but his bantering manner keeps people at a distance. I've seen Mom flare up when he backs off from things, always joking. But with Peter's father you really feel his presence in an immediate, tactile way. I'd wondered way before this summer why such a handsome man married a mousy, quiet woman like Peter's mother, whether she was "enough" for him. Evidently not, from what Peter says. I wonder if Mom knows she's not the first.

When I got back home to our summer house, Daddy was lying in the hammock reading an old issue of *Gourmet*. He used to cook a lot on vacation since he doesn't have time to during the year, but this vacation he hasn't so much. One odd thing about Daddy is that he likes to just read recipes. Even for things he isn't going to cook. He says it keeps him from eating so much. You'd think it would be the opposite, that it would make him hungrier, but he says no, that reading about cooking makes him feel he's done it, maybe the way pornography works for people who have hang-ups about sex.

Suddenly he looked forlorn and pale to me lying there, probably only because of what I know about Mom and Peter's father. I went over and gave him a kiss.

"Hi, sweets," he said, looking up. "How's the beach?"

"Good. Do you want to do the shopping now?"

"Maybe we'd better— Oh, by the way, your mother called. She'll be back a day later than she expected, so we'll just have to forage for ourselves."

I swallowed. A flash image of Mom and Nelson went through my mind. "That's okay," I said brightly. "It doesn't matter. I guess it's sort of lonely for you, though."

"I'll survive," he said with his funny smile.

"Would you like fish again?" I said.

"Why not? I'm in a fairly fishy mood. But I'm amenable to other suggestions."

I wonder if Daddy would disapprove if he knew about Peter and me. He's liberal in his ideas, but he might be more conservative when it comes to his own daughter. We've always been extremely close. He was the one who explained sex to me, whom I discussed personal things with, so I always assumed I'd tell him when I was finally doing it. But I feel as though this is too private. I don't want to tell anyone. "Was Mom one of the first people you really liked?" I asked.

"Girls?"

"I mean, how did it begin? Right off when you first saw her?"

"Actually I believe that in our particular case your mother, for reasons which I must admit are a little obscure to me, developed a 'thing' for me. And of course I was flattered."

"Didn't you develop a 'thing' for her?"

"Well, I wouldn't have had the courage to do that unless I knew the other person felt something. Let that be an object lesson to you, darling."

Daddy is very verbal—he talks a lot and has a huge vocabulary, yet it's hard to know what he feels about things. He and Mom don't fight, for instance, or at least she sometimes yells while he just sits there, looking as though it were a play he didn't find sufficiently entertaining. Would he be devastated if he knew about Mom and Nelson? I just have no idea.

"Mira does funny things sometimes," I said. "You know what she did last summer?"

"Can't guess."

"She found her mother's diary and read parts of it."

"That does sound nasty," Daddy said.

"She knew she shouldn't . . . but she said it was like she couldn't help herself."

"Well, I trust she was rewarded by finding out something sufficiently unpleasant."

"In a way."

"Other people's secrets aren't usually that interesting, though," Daddy said. "I've never understood the point of diaries."

"Didn't you ever keep one?"

"Never."

"Remember, when I was little, I had that dream diary where I wrote all my dreams?"

"Yes, but that was different. As I recall, you used to come in every morning and read what you'd written. It was intended for public consumption. In fact, it made me very jealous."

"How come?"

"You seemed to have such delightful adventures every time your head touched the pillow. It didn't seem fair. I hardly ever dream at all. I guess I'd be a bad case for an analyst."

"I don't dream so much anymore," I said to console him.

He patted my hand. "Good. I forgive you, then. By the way, did you see Peter Galing? He called earlier."

"Yes, I saw your note."

"He should come around for another game of chess. I think I could give him a pretty stiff fight this time."

"I wish I played chess better."

"You're too much of a daydreamer, sweetheart. You don't want to win enough."

"I think I do. I feel like I'm trying to."

"A little more tenacity."

I thought of Peter. "Peter doesn't seem like he'd have more tenacity than me."

"Oh, I believe he has. With parents like that he's had to, I imagine."

"Like what?"

"Well, of course I may be wrong, but I always felt they were rather absorbed in the two oldest boys—I forget their names—and Peter had to fend for himself pretty much. Not that I don't like him much the best. The other two—why can't I remember their names—Nelson was so proud of them, and I never could see why."

I wonder what Daddy really thinks of Peter's parents. I've always had the feeling that he looks down on Peter's father as not being intellectual enough but is fond, in a mild way, of Peter's mother.

"I believe we're due to see the Galings this coming week," Daddy said. "Well, your mother has it on the calendar, at any rate. Dinner, perhaps. So, where's that grocery list? Do we have everything written down?"

I went into the kitchen, which is sort of small, and got the list. Anyone who thinks they need something writes it down, and then we put it on our list on the days we go to the store. Actually I like going shopping with Daddy. He says shopping appeals to his sense of order. He doesn't like just stopping at the store to pick up things on impulse, the way Mom does, or buying odds and ends. On Fire Island we have a special round of places we go to. While Daddy was shopping in the first store, I stood and looked down the beach front.

Suddenly I saw Peter's Uncle Morgan. I hadn't seen him so far this summer. He'd gotten extremely thin! He's Peter's father's brother. Peter likes him, I think. He comes and stays with them every summer.

"Greetings, my good man," Morgan said when Daddy came outside. "Where have you been hiding yourself?"

"He's just been loafing," I said, "lying in a hammock."

"Just as I suspected," Morgan said.

"You see the cruelty of the young," Daddy said. "Here I am, holding up the household, making lists, being a mainstay, and it's called loafing. I ask you, where is the justice in this world?"

"That's something I've been meaning to ask *you*," Morgan said.

"Avoid the young," Daddy said. "That's my advice. They are intemperate and hasty in their judgments."

"Oh, Daddy," I said. "I didn't really—"

"No denials," Daddy said. "I have a witness here. Morgan, did you or did you not hear this otherwise charming young lady accuse me of being a loafer?"

"I did," Morgan said. "It grieves me very much to say it, but I did."

"I can see that it grieves you," Daddy said, "and I appreciate that. . . . So how long will you be around?"

"The usual."

"Forgive me, but I forget how long the usual is."

"Ten days. That's all they give me. I prefer to take the other week in the winter."

"Sounds most luxurious to me," Daddy said.

"Luxurious, no, but it breaks up the year."

"An essential thing—breaking up the year," Daddy said. "Well, I believe we'll be seeing you the day after tomorrow. Aline has something on her calendar about dinner with the Galings."

"Oh, but I fear—"

"Does dinner with us lead to fears?"

"I believe Hope said that Nelson is going to be detained in the city for a day or so. He's gone in for work, poor fellow."

"These workaholics are a disgrace," Daddy said. "We'll have to do something to stop them."

"I quite agree."

"So we've been canceled, scratched from the agenda?"

"No, I think . . . Hope was saying she hoped you'd come anyway."

"Hope hoped . . . Well, if Hope hoped, one cannot let that hope go unmet. What do you say, Les?"

"I'd like to come," I said, wondering if Mom would be back by then. "But, Daddy, we should finish our shopping."

"Of course we should. Why are we standing here idling away our time in this disgraceful manner? I blame it all on this gentleman. Gentleman, do you accept the blame?"

"I do," Morgan said. "I will take my humble purchases and depart. . . . See you then."

Daddy raised his hand in parting. Daddy talks that way a lot, but when he's with someone like Peter's Uncle Morgan, he can do it forever. I think it gets Mom irritated at times. We bought all our things and loaded them in the wagon.

"Daddy?"

"What, sweets?"

"Morgan looked so thin. Didn't he? To you?"

"Yes, he did," Daddy said.

"I wonder why."

"He's dying," Daddy said.

I stared at him. "How do you know?"

"He has cancer. He's had it for a few years, but I gather it's in a more advanced stage now."

I wondered how he could just stand around and joke like that with Daddy if it was true. "Maybe he'll get better," I said.

"No," Daddy said. "This'll be his last summer."

I took Daddy's hand. "I like him."

"I do too."

"It doesn't seem fair."

"It isn't.

"Do you think he knows?"

"Most likely."

"I don't know how he can just go around like that, shopping and everything, knowing."

"What's his alternative?" He frowned. "It upsets me partly because I had a good friend at college, William McGill, who died of a very similar kind of thing."

I was surprised. Daddy had never mentioned that. "Was he someone you were very close to?"

"Very. It happened with tremendous suddenness."

My mind flashed to Mom and Peter's father, my finding the diary. *It happened with tremendous suddenness.* I reached out and took Daddy's arm and held it tightly against me as we walked back to the cottage.

Close Encounters of the Fourth Kind

"Do you think they noticed when we left?" Leslie said. She was sitting cross-legged on the bed. We had snuck off to her parents' cottage after the dinner Mom gave for Uncle Morgan and Leslie's father, and we had been in bed for almost an hour.

"They might have noticed," I said. "But I don't think they suspected anything."

"I thought I saw your mother smile at your uncle."

"She always does. They get along. It's weird, but they get along much better than Mom and Dad."

"Maybe she should have married your uncle instead."

"Then he wouldn't be my uncle."

"Then you wouldn't even have been born! . . . I wonder where Mom and your father are now. I wonder if she takes him home to our place or what."

"It's because of Uncle Morgan that Dad met Mom," I said.

"How come?"

"Well, they were in some English class together at college, and they started getting friendly."

"Has your uncle ever been married?"

"Uh-uh. I don't think he's the type."

"Is your cramp okay now, Peter?"

I'd gotten a cramp in my leg just at the end of our lovemaking. It didn't help the mood any, having to get up and go hopping around like a kangaroo, but I couldn't help it. "I think it's better," I said. I had my shirt and slacks on again because I still feel a little funny having Leslie stare at me when I'm naked. If I were in better shape, I wouldn't mind.

"I can massage it for you if you want," she said. "Come on, lie down."

Obediently I lay down on her bed, my head on the pillow, and Leslie began rubbing and pulling at the part of my leg where I'd had the cramp. "That feels good," I said.

"Well, if nothing else works out, I can always get a job at a massage parlor when I graduate college."

"I thought you wanted to be an actress. Don't you?"

"Yeah, I do, but it might take a long time till I get real parts. You have to audition for them, like your father does for commercials."

"Dad used to want to be an actor," I said. "Mom always says I shouldn't mention it because he's sensitive about the fact that it didn't pan out and all he does is commercials."

"You mean he wanted to be a serious actor and do Shakespeare and things like that?"

"Yeah. Uncle Morgan did too. He still acts. That's how he makes a living."

"I didn't know that," Leslie said. "Maybe I'll ask him about it sometime."

I turned over. "The way I see it, Dad is jealous of Uncle Morgan because he thinks he looks down on him for doing commercials, and Uncle Morgan is jealous of Dad because he makes lots of money."

Leslie rested her head on my shoulder. "Peter, Daddy said your uncle is very sick. Is he?"

"Yeah, I gather he is. He had a lot of chemotherapy last year, and it worked for a while, but—"

"Would you want to know if you had something incurable?"

"I'm not sure," I said. I've thought about that. I think it's great that some people really want to know and can face it, but I'm not positive I'm one of them. It makes me feel awful being with Uncle Morgan. He's such a nice guy, so much nicer than my father.

"I would want to know," Leslie said. "Basically I'm a coward, but I'd still rather know the truth."

It seemed morbid to be lying there after sex talking about dying. "Hey, Les, let's get something to eat, okay?"

She sat up. "Should I bring you something? Some cake and milk, or fruit if we have some? We have pound cake." A few minutes later she returned with a slice of cake and a glass of milk. She was eating a peach.

"That's all you're having?" I said.

"I love peaches." Leslie looked very cute in her T-shirt and bikini underpants, like a sexy elf.

"No wonder you're so skinny," I said, teasing.

"Am I? Much too skinny? I think I'm not as bad as I was."

"Listen, you're lucky to be skinny. Look at me!"

"You just have a thing about being fat," Leslie said. "You're perfect."

I guess it's hard not to fall for a girl who either truly believes that or can lie so effortlessly. "Well, I don't exactly—" Before I could finish my sentence, we heard something out in the hall. "Oh, my God," Leslie whispered.

"Should I go out and see who it is?"

Leslie looked down. "No, I'll go." Her voice was still very low. She stood up and slipped a nightgown over her head.

"Anybody home?" a feminine voice called out.

Leslie sucked in her breath. "It's Mom," she whispered. "Oh, Jesus. She said she wouldn't be back till tomorrow. Listen, stay here while I go out and speak to her, okay?"

I didn't think I had much choice. I lay back, my stomach contracting.

"Oh, hi, Mom," I heard Leslie say.

"Leslie! I thought no one was here. It was so quiet."

"Daddy's at the Galings playing Scrabble with Peter's mother and uncle."

"Oh, I'm glad," Leslie's mother said. "I'm always afraid that when I'm away, Preston doesn't have any social life. How've things been? I'm sorry I couldn't get back sooner."

"Oh, they've been fine," Leslie said. "Maybe you could go over and have coffee with them or something."

"I couldn't," Leslie's mother said. "I'm totally beat. I think I'll just take a shower and pop right into bed. We can talk in the morning."

"I'm glad you're back, Mom."

"I'm glad to be back. Sleep tight, sweetie."

A minute later Leslie came quietly back into the room. "Close encounters of the fourth kind," she said.

"I'd better get back," I said, sitting up.

"Peter, I'm sorry. I really didn't expect her to—"

"It's okay, don't worry about it . . . That was a good massage before. And, well, the other part too."

I left the house quietly.

It's not a long walk from Leslie's house to the one my parents own. I like walking along the beach at night, even when it's overcast, like tonight. I wonder if I'm a good lover to Leslie. She never says exactly how it is for her, and that could mean anything, that I'm doing it too fast or whatever. One reason I do it a little fast is I'm afraid she'll change her mind in the middle.

When I got back, they were watching the TV news.

"Who won?" I asked.

"Hope," Leslie's father said. "It was a disgrace for the men tonight, a true and unequivocal comedown."

"You're giving up so soon?" Uncle Morgan said. "I demand a rematch at once."

"At once is too soon," Leslie's father said. "My brain is benumbed at this hour of the night . . . Peter, my dear Peter, where is my glorious daughter? What have you done with her?"

I know that's just the way Leslie's father talks, but it made me nervous, given what I had, in fact, just done. "I just, uh, walked her home," I stammered. "We took a walk on the beach."

"That's nice, Peter," Mom said. She squinted at me. "Darling, I think you're overdoing the sun. Doesn't he look awfully pink?"

"A mere rosy glow, natural to youth," Leslie's father said.

"He looks a little sunburned. Peter, take my sun cream if you like."

I shook my head. "It doesn't hurt, Mom, seriously."

"Look, there's Nelson," Uncle Morgan said.

We all turned to the TV to see Dad come marching up to take care of some insurance claim for someone. He was wearing a three-piece pinstriped suit, which in real life Dad would never wear. He didn't even speak until the end, when he kind of put his arm around the mother and father and said: "We'll take care of you. That's our business."

"I like that one," Mom said reflectively.

"My favorite is the paper towel test," Uncle Morgan said.

"Morgan, don't be sarcastic about it. It's what Nelson does, and he does it well. Isn't that all that counts?"

"Not in my book," Uncle Morgan said. "What do you say, Peter?"

"He seems pretty good at it," I said. "I never saw him act in a regular play, so I can't tell exactly."

"You see," Mom said, "if Nelson had gone into straight acting, like you, Morgan, he wouldn't have made it. I think it took courage for him to admit that to himself."

"He doesn't admit it, though," Uncle Morgan said. "That's what I object to. He talks as though doing this kind of idiocy were on the same plane as being in the theater."

"Well, with you he's jealous. That's different."

Uncle Morgan gave a hollow laugh. "Jealous? Of me?"

"Of course he is," Mom said. "You must know that."

"Why isn't anyone jealous of me?" Leslie's father put in. "I want someone to be jealous of me?"

"Sure," I said. "What should I be jealous about?"

"My beauty, my wit, my ravishing daughter."

I thought of Leslie and me in bed together and couldn't look him in the eye. I wonder how he'd feel if he knew.

"Okay," I said. "I'm jealous of all that."

"And now is he satisfied?" Uncle Morgan said. "No, he is not."

"Speak for yourself, my good fellow. I certainly *am* satisfied," Leslie's father said. "You see before you a man glowing with inner satisfaction, all owing to this considerate young man."

"I think Leslie looks so much more . . . grown up this summer," my mother said. "Don't you think so, Peter?"

I tried to seem detached. "She looks pretty much the same to me."

"Maybe it's that new hairstyle. It's really very becoming to her. If I had the courage, I'd wear my hair that way." Mom has brownish-grayish hair which is loose around her shoulders. She has a pleasant, round face with friendly blue eyes, but it's more her character that's appealing. People always like to tell her their secrets.

"Mom, don't cut your hair that short," I said. "It would look awful."

Mom put up a hand. "I won't. But I do think that on

Leslie it's very becoming . . . Oh, dear, I'm afraid we missed *Anna Karenina*."

"Were we expecting her?" Leslie's father said.

"On TV. It started at ten."

"Oh, well, you can still watch," Uncle Morgan said. "Isn't the beginning just about how she meets whatever-his-name-is?"

I went into the kitchen to get another glass of milk. It seems to me that I am always thirsty after we make love. I decided to go into the bedroom and call Leslie. It took three rings for her to answer.

"Hi," I said. "It's me. I just called to say good night."

"I'm glad you called," she said sleepily.

"Is your mother asleep?"

"Her door's closed. I think she probably is. I can't stop thinking about her and your father."

"Just don't worry about it so much. . . . Les?"

"Yeah?"

"That was good tonight . . . being with you."

"Yes, it was," Leslie said, but she sounded a little subdued.

"We don't have to do it every time we get together," I said. "Just whenever you feel in the mood."

"I *think* I was in the mood," Leslie said. "It's just I was a little . . . I kept thinking about how this will end, with Mom and you father."

"Sure, I understand."

"Were you in the mood?"

"Um-hum." But I think I would almost always be in the mood if I knew she wanted to.

"Thanks for calling, Peter. Talking to you makes me feel better."

"See you in the morning?"

"Right. Sleep well."

The Big Day

THE DAY AFTER MOM RETURNED FROM THE CITY WAS THE calm before the storm. Everything seemed suspiciously quiet, held in. What really clued me in was that she and Daddy went off and had dinner together alone, not taking me. Normally the three of us would go together, especially if she'd been away for a while. I fell asleep before they came back, despite being nervous.

The next morning when I got up, Mom was already in the kitchen squeezing orange juice. "It's such a lovely day," she said. "Why don't we take a walk on the beach, Les. Do you feel like it?"

Our eyes met, and I knew it wasn't going to be an ordinary walk. My stomach tightened. "Sure," I said. "Just let me get into my suit."

Mom was in her usual one-piece blue tank suit. She's in excellent shape—works out at a gym near the brokerage house where she works, eats healthy things. Everyone says she looks at least ten years younger than she really is; it's true. She had a towel draped around her shoulders. With her sunglasses on I couldn't see her expression that well.

We both had a quick swim and then walked along the beach. Mom said, "Hon, Dad and I had a long talk last night," she began, "about you."

"What about me?" I'd decided to play totally innocent no matter what.

"I don't know how to say this to make it any easier, even though I've been thinking about it for ages." She glanced at me. "We're going to get a divorce."

I was silent for a moment. "I'm sorry," I said.

"You don't need me to say we both love you and want, more than anything, not to unsettle your life, especially since you only have one more year of school till college. I would've waited, but—"

"That's okay," I said. Even though I'd known what was coming, the whole conversation was awful, worse than I'd expected. I didn't want to make it easy for her. I felt angry. "Who will I be living with?"

"With whoever you like." She hesitated. "Basically we thought that you could live with me but stay over with Daddy whenever you felt like it."

"Do you know where you'll be living yet?"

There was a long pause.

"There's another part of this, Les. It's . . . well, it isn't just the divorce. I—I've fallen in love with someone, and, well, we're going to get married as soon as the divorce becomes final."

"Congratulations," I said.

She looked at me. "Don't you want to know who it is?"

"Who is it?"

"It's someone I've known a very long time. We haven't been . . . We didn't fall in love right away. It was more a gradual . . . It's Nelson Galing."

"Peter's father?"

"Yes. I know how fond you and Peter have always been of each other. You'll have a brother, finally."

"That's nice," I said sarcastically. "He's really good-looking, Nelson."

Evidently Mom was choosing to ignore my tone. "Isn't he? You know, it's funny. I've never liked conventionally handsome men, they always seemed so full of themselves, but Nelson is so—he's such an exciting, intense person. I feel like my world has come alive suddenly. Can you understand that?"

"Sure. What does Daddy think?"

"Well, you know your father. Sometimes, I wonder how much he really needs people. Oh, deep down of course he must, and naturally he adores you, but it's all so buried. That's been very hard for me. I'm a much more emotional person. I just needed more. It isn't anyone's fault."

"No."

Finally Mom turned and said, "I think you're mad at me, Les."

Very observant, Mom. "Not really. It's your life."

"It's your life too. Come on, let it out. Yell at me."

"Why should I?"

"I'm changing things, I'm wrecking your life. You won't see Daddy so much."

"I don't mind," I said.

"Les, for Christ's sake, be honest."

"Well, okay. I wish you were still in love with Daddy. I think it's a shitty thing to do to him."

"Not loving him the way I once did?"

"Yeah. You loved him in the beginning, didn't you?"

"I think so," Mom said. "In the beginning seems so long ago."

"Is that why I'm an only child, because you stopped loving him?" I asked. We both had our sunglasses on, and

Mom's screened her face, so I could hardly see her eyes. Everything looked greenish gold.

"No. I had two miscarriages after I had you. And then I figured why go on trying?"

"So, I almost wasn't an only child?"

"Right. The second miscarriage came when I was in my fifth month. That was a real killer."

Even though we were talking about something that must have been depressing at the time, Mom looked so cheerful and happy that it was like it had happened to someone else.

"Was Daddy the first person you slept with?" I asked. I'd always wondered about that, and now seemed as good a time as any to ask.

"No. I'm sorry."

"What're you sorry about?"

"Well, I have the feeling you'd like to think he was the first."

"No. I don't want to think that. Because then you might have married him just to sleep with him."

"Not I, said the little red hen. I was always practical about sex, not especially romantic . . . until now. Now, with Nelson, I feel—well, differently. All that crap about I will love you forever seems to make sense."

I smiled stiffly. "That's nice."

"What amazes me about Nelson is how much he knows about things. And he doesn't have any vanity about it either. I think you're going to love him, Les, once you get to know him better."

"He's sexy," I conceded.

"Oh, isn't he! Listen, I had to beat off quite a few would-be girl friends to get to him. I feel like my life is starting over. It's a terrific feeling."

"Lots of kids in my class have parents who're divorced," I said.

"It's so much healthier," Mom said. "I just don't see the

point of living a life with nothing in it but pretense. What's the point? We'll look for an apartment with a lovely room for you. You can decorate it from scratch, however you like."

"I like my own room," I said.

"Sure. Well, you'll still have it. You'll visit Daddy as often as you want."

I started thinking about Daddy's harpsichords. He bought one from a friend a long time ago, and then he decided to build his own. For almost a year all the pieces were spread out on the floor, but he finally did build it. Mom kept yelling that our living room had no place to walk around in, that we were being "overrun" by harpsichords. "Was it because of the harpsichords?" I asked suddenly.

"Was what because of the harpsichords?"

"You always used to seem so mad at Daddy about that."

"Oh, darling, the harpsichords are the tip of the iceberg. But it's true—look at the way we were living!"

Just then I saw Peter. He'd been out sailing and was bringing the boat onto the sand. I wondered if his father had broken the news yet.

"Hi, Peter!" Mom said very cheerfully. "Did you have a good sail?"

"Pretty good. The wind is funny today. It keeps starting up and then dying down."

"Come in for a swim with us. Maybe you can persuade Leslie. I don't seem to have any effect on her." She stood up and looked at Peter, her head to one side in a way she has.

"I guess I'll just sit in the sun," Peter said. "You go in, Les."

"Uh-uh. I went in before."

"Well, I want another go at it," Mom said. "Sure you won't join me, Peter?"

"No, thanks, Mrs. Hertz."

Peter and I sat side by side, looking at Mom going into the water.

"What's happening with *your* parents?" I said. "She just told me officially."

"Mom's crying. Dad took off like a shot after telling Mom she'd have to sell our house in Westport and move into a smaller house or something. I think that's one of the things that got her upset."

"Your house *is* kind of big." They have a huge three-story Victorian-style house. We used to go there at Christmas sometimes.

"They used to talk about moving, but now I guess it seems to Mom like she's being forced out," said Peter.

"I hate it when my mother flirts with you," I said suddenly, watching her swim way out in the water. "I really hate it! Why doesn't she act her age?"

"She was just being friendly."

"She never acts that way with me. It's phony!"

"Probably she feels funny with me. I can see that."

"Peter, you're so understanding about everything. Cut it out! Don't you even feel upset?"

"Sure, I do. What'd you think? It made it a little easier for me that I was prepared, that's all."

"For me that doesn't seem to matter much. I don't know why. . . . She's just so perky and happy, as though Daddy and I don't count for anything."

Peter was silent. "Well, there's not a lot we can do about it."

I felt better after my outburst, even though it seemed absurd to have let it out on Peter. "Lie down, let me put some of this suntan stuff on you. You're all pink," I told him.

"That's just the way I get."

"Come on, lie down. It'll feel good."

Peter lay down on his stomach, and I began rubbing his

shoulders. "It makes me feel horny when you do that," he said.

"It does, huh?" I kept rubbing.

"Les, I mean it. I don't feel like developing an erection right now."

"I thought you said it was a good feeling."

"At the right time and in the right place."

I lay down next to him on the towel. Our noses were almost touching. Peter stuck his tongue out and put it against my nose. "Salty," he said.

I touched my tongue to his nose. "Hmmm, I don't know. Maybe peppermint."

"A peppermint nose?"

"Yeah, why not? . . . So, is your father staying for the rest of the summer?"

"I don't think so. He packed some stuff and said he was going to a motel."

I felt some cold drops of water on my back. It was Mom, standing over us, shaking her head to get it dry. "Peter, you're going to get a terrible burn," she said.

"It's okay," he said. "Leslie put some of that stuff on me."

"You shouldn't have gone sailing. That sun is murder."

"I'll be okay," Peter said. He sat up. "I'll see you," he said, and ambled off.

I know Peter doesn't want Mom to know about us, but for some reason I felt hurt at the way he just walked off so casually.

"Why doesn't Hope make that boy lose ten pounds!" Mom said. "She bakes all those sweet things, and look at him! I mean, it doesn't matter now, but eventually he's going to get interested in girls, and who's going to want him?"

"He did lose some," I said. God, I hate the way Mom talks about Peter! What stupid values!

"They ignore that child," Mom went on. "Everything is

the first two. Cliff and Ken, that's all Nelson talks about! It's sweet that you can talk to him, Leslie."

"I—I think he's the nicest boy I've ever met," I stammered.

But Mom didn't seem to have heard. "Wait a sec. Is that Nelson?" She ran down to the edge of the water and came back with him a few moments later.

"Hi, Leslie," Nelson said. "How goes it?"

"It goes okay," I said wryly. He looked pleased with himself and the world, like he hadn't an iota of guilt about anything.

"Isn't it a fantastic day?" he said, looking all around. Mom stood next to him with her arm around his waist. They really did look like a couple in one of those ads you see for new houses or cars. "I see you've been in the water," he said, turning to Mom.

"Twice," Mom said, smiling at him. I felt sharply and uncomfortably aware of the sexual connection between them. They couldn't keep their hands off each other. I wonder if Peter and I are that obvious.

"I'm going to go in," he said. "Want to come, Ali?"

I never heard anyone call my mother Ali before.

"I don't know," she said. "Would you mind, Les?"

I shook my head.

"Just for a minute, then." They turned around and walked toward the ocean. I stood there awhile, and in a funny way I felt better. Seeing them side by side made them seem like a real couple.

When I came back, Daddy was alone in the house, sitting in the living room reading the newspaper. Suddenly I found myself flying into his arms, sobbing. I was amazed. I knew I'd been holding back with Mom, more out of numbness than anything else. Daddy hugged me and stroked my hair. "Sweetie, don't. It's going to be okay."

"How could she?" I said. "He's so awful!"

"It was inevitable," he said. "She needed someone more—"

"Do you feel terrible?" I pulled back to look at him. I'd been so concerned about my own feelings that I hadn't thought of what it must be like for him.

"I'll manage. Having you is all that counts."

"Mom said I'd be living mainly with her. Do I have to?"

"It's only for a year," Daddy said. "And we'll see each other as often as you like. There won't be any problem about that."

I wonder so much if Daddy had had any suspicions about what was going on before this. "Were you . . . surprised?" I said.

He shook his head. "Were you?"

I didn't feel, somehow, that I could mention the diary. If I hadn't found that, I would have been surprised. "You never fought that much. I never knew exactly what you felt."

"Well, I'm glad," he said. "I hate parents who make their private lives a battleground for their children. I wanted you to grow up with two parents who loved you. That's the reason we hung in there for so long."

I didn't say anything. And oddly I was glad that they had stayed together as long as they did. Even if it had been a sham, it'd been a convincing one.

The rest of the week Mom continued to be very friendly and cheerful, and Daddy was quiet. I tried to see Peter, but things were not so good at his house, and he couldn't get away that much.

One afternoon I walked over there on impulse. His mother was in the kitchen cleaning some clams. "Hi, Leslie," she said as I came in. "Peter's out sailing."

"Oh . . . Okay. Well, tell him I came around." I felt uncomfortable with her, as though I was responsible, somehow, for what she'd been going through.

"Have a seat. Help me with the clams."

"All right." I pulled up a stool next to her. "What are you going to make?"

"I thought of baking them with some bread crumbs and a little spinach. Morgan likes them that way."

"That sounds good."

"Do you cook much? I remember, when I was your age, I loved making cakes and cookies. I used to wreck the kitchen, but I really loved it."

"I used to make cookies," I said, "but I haven't for a long time."

"I have to get my weight under control," Peter's mother said. "Look at me! It's awful. It's no wonder Nelson—" Then all of a sudden she started to cry, right into the clams.

I felt bad. She's such a sweet person, though with none of Mom's charm or effervescence. I'm sure any man would understand Nelson's choice.

I didn't know exactly what to do. "Are you okay?" I said.

Peter's mother sniffed into her apron. "I'm getting impossible," she said. "I just swore that I would get through one whole day without crying, and I was so good this morning. I thought having a project, like the clams, would help."

I patted her shoulder. "I'm sorry, Mrs. Galing."

She looked up, red-eyed, at me. "I don't even know what to do! Give him a divorce, wait for it to blow over—I just don't *know.*"

She looked so desperate that I said, "Isn't there some lawyer or someone who could—"

"Oh, I *hate* lawyers!" she said. "I truly despise most of them. But you're right, I will get in touch with one. I was obviously crazily naïve to think that Nelson . . . Well, you know how handsome he is."

"Yes, he is," I said.

"It's a wonder it didn't happen sooner," she said. "That's the real mystery. Not that it happened now."

"Maybe you'll meet someone else," I said, trying to cheer her up.

"I'm not that type," she said. "The effort it takes for all of that is just beyond me. I can't even contemplate it."

"I didn't mean now," I said. "I meant just . . . maybe sometime."

"Sure, sometime," she repeated. "Let's keep up with the clams. . . . Leslie, did I tell you I like your hair short that way? It really is darling. I would have loved to wear my hair that way when I was your age, but my mother would have scalped me."

"Peter says it was better before," I said, glad she was over her crying fit.

"Peter! I wouldn't exactly call him an expert on girls. He's such a dear!" She sighed. "I'm so lucky to have Peter here now. Ken and Cliff would've been no help at all, but I feel like I can talk to Peter. I've always felt that way, even when he was a baby. He'd sit there so solemnly and look at me, and he was just— No, but I don't want to use him. That would be bad."

"I don't think you're using him exactly," I said.

"Well." She looked thoughtful. "I just don't know. . . . Oh, and the house! It must be my mood, but when I think of anything, you name it, I just feel like throwing my hands up in despair. Everything seems so overwhelming. Do you know that feeling?"

"Sort of," I said.

"It's good that it's now, though," she went on. "If it had been ten years ago, with all three boys at home . . . No, I guess that was considerate of Nelson, waiting for the right moment. Do you think they'll be happy together?"

I shrugged. "I guess so."

"I always used to think opposites attract, but it seems to

me that Nelson and Aline are just alike. They're both totally self-centered egomaniacs with a hell of a lot of charm. . . . Well, that's unfair, I guess."

It seemed fair to me. "No, I think—" But as I was shelling the last clam, the knife slipped, and I cut myself. The blood started running onto the butcher block table. Peter's mother jumped up. "Here, wrap this around it," she said. She handed me a dishtowel. "I hope we have Band-Aids."

It didn't hurt that much, but I hated seeing the blood going into the dish towel. Peter's mother came back with some gauze and a big flat Band-Aid, which she wrapped tightly around my finger. "How does it feel now?" she asked.

"It doesn't hurt," I said truthfully.

"Leslie, you know, I hope we won't lose touch now that . . . I mean, I always had a fantasy of having a daughter, and I used to imagine that if I had had one, she would have been like you."

I tried to smile. I started thinking how I wouldn't have minded Peter's mother being mine. She's so much easier to talk with than my mother is. Just the way she broke down, the way she shared her feelings with me. I don't feel Mom ever really does that. "I think we'll still see each other," I told her.

"Sometimes I come in for plays or movies," she said, moving the bowl of clams to one side and sponging up the streaks of blood. "We could go together. Would you like to?"

"Sure," I said.

I stayed until she had finished fixing the rest of the clams. I wondered how Peter would feel about my talking to his mother about such personal things.

Girl Friends

PETER, THERE'S ONE THING I WANT TO SAY TO YOU." UNCLE Morgan had finished packing his bags and was stuffing a magazine into his briefcase. "Your father is a son of a bitch."

"No," Mom said from the other room. "He isn't, Morgan. Don't say that."

"I'll say it till the cows come home. I'll put it in skywriting. It's the truth."

"He has a right to his own life," Mom said. "That's everyone's right."

"Nope," said Uncle Morgan. "Not when it affects other people, women and children."

"Peter's not a child," Mom said, just as I was about to protest.

"He's a youth, then," Morgan said. "A comparative youth."

"Mom and I'll be okay," I said to reassure him.

"How can she send her daughter over here at a time like this is beyond me," Uncle Morgan went on, "simply beyond my powers of comprehension."

"You mean Leslie?" I said. "She just came around to see me."

"Yes, Morgan, really. She's Peter's friend. She's certainly not responsible."

"Preston is the only one in that family I would really trust," Uncle Morgan said.

"I wonder how Preston is taking it," Mom said.

"Leslie said he seems very calm," I said.

"Well, I'm sure he doesn't cry his head off every day like some idiots around here," Mom said scornfully. "He has more sense."

Uncle Morgan went over and touched her on the shoulder. "You have sense, Hope," he said.

"About what?" Mom said suddenly. "Name one sensible thing I've done in my whole life!"

"Peter."

"Okay. That's not a very long list."

"You're being too hard on yourself," he said. "Peter, don't let her be that way."

They started talking about getting together in the city. I went back to my room to read till Uncle Morgan was ready to go. I was planning to walk him to the dock where he got his boat. As we were leaving, Mom called out, "Peter, remember, your father's coming around at six to take you out to dinner."

"I won't forget, Mom," I said. I took Uncle Morgan's suitcase. He didn't look quite so pale as he had earlier in the summer, but he was still awfully skinny. I wonder how much longer he'll live.

"Peter," he said as we were walking along the shore, "I meant what I said about your mother. You take good care of her."

"I will," I said, though I wasn't sure exactly what he meant or how I was supposed to do that.

"What bothers me," he went on, "is that it's all my fault. Why did I introduce them? But at the time I remember thinking that they were so unalike, they wouldn't even make it through a first date. That doesn't say much for my powers of judgment."

"Mom's still in love with him, I think," I said. The suitcase was getting heavy, so I switched it to the other hand.

"I'm afraid that's so," Uncle Morgan said. "But if you can fall in, you can fall out. . . . I remember the first person I was ever in love with. She never even knew about it, but I felt like I was going through the seventh circle of the damned. Have you ever felt like that?"

"Uh-uh." I thought about Leslie, but sometimes it's more like we're just friends who're sleeping together than that we have a grand passion of the kind Uncle Morgan seemed to mean.

"I wish I lived closer to you," Uncle Morgan said. "It might be a comfort to Hope, but I could never live out there, the way you do. Maybe you'll move in once this is all settled."

"To the city?" I'd never thought about our doing that. I wasn't sure I liked the idea.

"It's an option," Uncle Morgan said. Then he turned and said, "Preston!"

It was Leslie's father taking a walk. He looked startled when Uncle Morgan called his name. "What, leaving this earthly paradise so soon?" he said.

"Duty calls," Uncle Morgan said.

"A slave to duty. Poor fellow." Leslie's father smiled. "We'll miss you at Scrabble."

"You'll stay on till the end of the month?" Uncle Morgan said.

"Till the bitter end," Leslie's father said.

"I'm . . . sorry about what happened," Uncle Morgan said.

'Oh, that. A mere trifle," Leslie's father said. "Life goes on despite these trifles."

"Yes, but—"

"And Hope, the fair Hope, how is she faring?"

"Crying," I said. "A lot."

Leslie's father looked concerned. "Oh, dear. Yes, well, that was to be expected."

"She seemed better today," I said.

"I worry about her," Uncle Morgan said. "I wish I could stay."

But his boat was coming in, and we had to hurry to get to the dock in time. I stood watching as it sailed away. From now on I'll be alone with Mom in the house, something that makes me a little uneasy. I'm all she has left, but I don't really feel I can make it up to her for what my father has done. I'd started looking forward to this year, coming into the city to see Leslie. Now I'm afraid Mom'll want me around to keep her company. I walked back to our cottage as slowly as possible, hoping she might have gone for a walk or something. I didn't feel like seeing Dad that night either. All of a sudden, after not having been the least bit friendly for years, he seemed to be trying to make up for lost time and do a real father-son number, which struck me as completely phony.

When I got home, Mom was coming out of the shower. Her hair was wrapped in a turban. "He got away all right?" she said. "Peter, take a shower before you go out with your father. I don't think you've been near water in days."

In fact, I'd showered a couple of times at Leslie's house after we made love, but I decided not to mention that. "Sure, only I don't see why I have to bend over backward to impress him."

"It's not bending over backward. It's just that I want him to see that we're managing well by ourselves."

As I showered, I looked down at my body. It didn't look as bad to me as it usually did, maybe because Leslie approves of it. I knew I could lose some weight, but I felt more solid, not blubbery the way I used to when I was a kid. I decided I would try not to eat that much when Dad took me out.

He came right on time, at six. I'd been sitting on the porch, looking at a copy of *People* which Uncle Morgan had left behind. Mom had disappeared into her bedroom.

"Hi, Peter!" Dad said. He can have a very cheerful manner, but I've rarely seen him turn it on me.

"Hi," I said.

"So what do you feel like having on our big night out? I guess it's Chinese or Italian."

I know Italian food is fattening, but I love it, so I said, "Italian."

Dad looked around. "Where is everybody?"

"Uncle Morgan went home this afternoon, and Mom's lying down or something."

"Oh, damn, I forgot about Morgan's having to leave so early. I'll give him a call later."

I suddenly felt like telling him that Uncle Morgan thought he was a son of a bitch, but I didn't. I wonder why I can't talk about anything with Dad. I can even talk to Mom better than to him. Every time I think of something to say, it sounds stupid.

I ordered lasagna at the restaurant, and Dad had a martini and veal marsala. While we were waiting for the food, he said, "I realize this may sound a bit insincere, but I'm sorry about everything that's happened, Peter."

"That's okay," I said.

"I would have waited until you were in college, but these things have their own timetable. If it was just an affair, that would be different, but I really want to marry Aline and have a home with her. I think when you get to know her, you'll understand why."

"She seems pretty nice," I said.

"She's more than nice," he said. "She's just—well, she's easily the most resourceful person I've ever met. Preston just couldn't keep up with her."

"Who were the other ones?" I said all of a sudden, "before her."

Dad looked uncomfortable. "Other what?" he said.

"Girl friends." Somehow, now that I had one of my own, it seemed easier to talk about it with him.

For a second I thought Dad was going to deny there had been any others, but he said, "Only one of them really meant anything to me, and she ended up marrying someone else."

"Was she married too?"

"No . . . Listen, don't be a baby, Peter. You know this kind of thing is common. Everyone does it. Hope and I just aren't suited to each other. That's all there is to it. . . . How's *your* social life going?"

"Me?" I felt embarrassed. "It's going okay, I guess."

"At your age it's all fun and games," he said. "When you're my age, things get trickier."

I bet if most adults were really young again, even for one day, they'd realize it isn't so easy at all. "I'll never be like Cliff," I said.

Dad smiled. "Yeah, Cliff has quite a line, doesn't he? I was surprised when he said he was settling down with that one girl."

The lasagna came, and I started eating.

"Don't gobble, Peter," Dad said irritably.

That hurt. I just wanted to eat before the food got cold. Anyway, I hadn't eaten any bread or ordered an appetizer. "I'm not gobbling," I said. "That's just the way I eat."

"I know the way you eat," he said, seeming annoyed. "It's too fast. Slow down. Look, if I gave up smoking, you can give up eating that way."

By now I almost didn't feel hungry, he was making such a big deal of it. I tried eating with deliberate slowness. "That okay?" I said sarcastically.

"Christ, you're what? Seventeen years old? It's a matter of manners. It's a matter of health. What girl is going to give you a tumble unless you get into shape? You know what I should really do?"

"What?"

"This winter I'm going to get you interested in squash. You'd feel a million times better."

"I'd rather swim."

"Swimming's okay, but what you need is something to get you moving around."

I felt so furious at him, I could hardly speak. What does he know? All he wants to do is criticize me. "Dad, would you lay off all my faults?"

"You *need* someone to get at you, Pete. Hope is so soft about everything."

"Leave Mom out of it too."

He was silent a moment. "Aren't you going to finish your lasagna?"

"Maybe in a minute." What I would have liked was to dump the whole thing on his head.

"Morgan's taking it hard," he said suddenly, as if he'd just thought of it.

"He didn't look that good this afternoon," I said. "Is he getting worse?"

"I'm afraid so. . . . We were really close when we were little, till college maybe. Then we sort of drifted apart. I think he resents my success."

"Mom says you resent him for not selling out."

I hoped that would get him, but he just said calmly,

"Selling out! Oh, dear." He looked away, then back at me. "How has your mother been taking it?"

"Crying a lot." *Feel guilty, you jerk!*

He frowned. "Well, she'll recover eventually. I hope I can get it through her head that staying on in that huge house is crazy. And I can't afford it."

"Where would we move to?"

"The city maybe. That way I could see you more, and, well, an apartment makes more sense when it's just two people. She doesn't need all that extra space now."

"But I'd have to leave school then, right in my senior year."

"All that can be worked out."

I didn't know whether or not to order dessert. I figured if I did, Dad would say something, so I just had a cup of coffee. When he saw me dumping sugar in it, he smiled. "I didn't get desert," I said defensively.

"Peter, Peter, Peter," Dad said.

"Dad, how old were you when you first had a real girl friend?"

"Oh, sixteen, seventeen, thereabouts. Why?"

"Who was the girl?"

"A friend of Morgan's. Hey, maybe there *is* a pattern there. I never thought of that. But he had good taste. He'd pick them, and I'd take them away."

"Is, uh, Leslie going to live with you?" I'd wanted to ask him that all evening but hadn't had the courage.

"Of course. Preston couldn't . . . Well, Aline feels Leslie belongs with her, and I agree. So you'll finally have a sister."

"Yeah, that'll be good," I said uncomfortably. The coffee felt hot as I swallowed it.

"I sometimes get the feeling you and Leslie don't hit it off that well."

"No, we do," I said hastily.

"She's a peculiar child, I think—high strung."

"Mom likes her," I said, wishing we could get on to another topic.

"Yes, she always did. Sympathy for the downtrodden."

"Dad, will you quit it? Leslie's not downtrodden."

"You know what I mean. She has that air of the lost waif—will someone give this underprivileged child a home?—that sort of thing."

"She's just kind of skinny."

But Dad didn't seem very interested in talking about Leslie.

"I'll be staying in the city," he said as he paid the check. "I think that's easier all around for everyone. But call me if you ever want to talk."

"Sure," I said. "I'll call."

PART II

The Wedding Party

THE WEDDING WAS AT CITY HALL. ALL THE "CHILDREN" were there: me, Peter, Cliff, all except Ken, Peter's middle brother, who's traveling in the Far East on a leave of absence from college. Mom looked pretty and young in a pale lavender dress with a lacy neckline. She held tightly to Nelson's arm. Although it was October, he still looked tan, the silver in his hair making it appear slightly gilded. I was wearing a new dress, in the old-fashioned style I like best with a long full skirt and a high neck. It was wine red. When I had modeled it for Daddy, he had said I looked Victorian. I wore an antique pin he had given me last Christmas, just to have a reminder of him with me. Peter wore a suit—it was the first time I could remember seeing him in one. It looked too tight, and he seemed uncomfortable.

During the ceremony I felt mainly detached and a little sad. I kept thinking of Daddy, whom I'd been with the day before, sitting at home alone, reading the Sunday paper. He's been as calm about the whole thing as he was when Mom first announced the news three months ago, but I feel that deep down he must mind. His life will be totally different now; and so will mine. But I've tried not to think ahead to that, to what it will be like afterward. It's all happened so quickly—Mom flying to Mexico for a quickie divorce, our moving into the new apartment. I decided just to try to survive the wedding.

The wedding party, which was huge, almost a hundred people, was held in the new apartment. It's on Central Park West and is so big that even with all those guests coming and going it didn't seem crowded. Maybe to assure numbness, I had a little too much to drink: three glasses of champagne, one after the other. I saw Peter watch me quaff the third glass. He smiled. "Better take it easy."

"Why? There's lots more." I gestured airily to the rows of bottles being poured by a hired man in a black coat.

"Well, have a good time, then."

"I'm trying to," I snapped. "I don't want to just stand around sneering at everything."

Peter flushed. "I'm not sneering," he said. "I just can't dance, and I hate all this noise."

"I'll show you. Come on." I tried dragging him onto the dance floor, but he pulled back. When Peter pulls, it's like you have a Saint Bernard on a leash; he's almost unmovable.

"I don't want to, Les, I mean it. Lay off."

"You'll like it if you try."

"Okay, maybe I would on some other occasion, but right now I'm not in the mood."

Of course I knew exactly what he was feeling because I was feeling the same way, but for some reason it got me furious the way he wouldn't even try. Things have been really strained between me and Peter ever since the summer ended. Even in August at Fire Island it wasn't the way it had been earlier in the summer. Daddy and I stayed until the end of the month, with Mom coming and going fairly often, but Peter and his mother went back to Westport. Peter doesn't write letters, and he's stiff on the phone. I've called him a few times, but it was like we were two people who'd been fixed up by well-meaning friends. I had to do all the work, and finally I felt fed up, disgusted, and secretly really hurt.

I hate it when they talk about a woman "giving herself" to a man. I want to think it's mutual, the giving part, but damn it, it *was* a big deal to me, making love with Peter, and I know he knows that. I also think it was a big deal for him—he said as much. So what's this all about? Awkwardness because now we're technically stepbrother and stepsister? Whatever it is, I just think it would help to talk about it. Okay, so Peter's shy and lacking in the social graces, but he's not exactly inarticulate. If he wants to break it off between us, for whatever reason, let him just say so. But I didn't quite have the heart to broach it so directly, especially at the party. I just turned on my heels and went off to dance with someone else.

I ended up with Peter's brother, Cliff. He's like a younger, more macho, but also more engaging version of Nelson—a real hunk, tan, athletic-looking, with curly hair to his shoulders, the kind of guy I usually think is a pain. He was wearing just jeans and a denim shirt with a gold chain around his neck, very California-looking. But he was a great dancer. I was conscious of Peter watching us from the sidelines and tried to act more carried away by the spirit of the occasion than I really felt.

"So you have three stepbrothers now," Cliff said when we stopped for a minute. The champagne I'd drunk made the room seem even bigger, like a huge whirling ball that kept tilting slightly to one side.

"I think it'll be fun," I said, looking up at him flirtatiously. I wondered if Peter had told him about us.

I saw my mother go over to Peter and talk with him. Mom looked sensational. Even though she's a redhead, she likes wearing clothes most red-haired people wouldn't think would suit them, like shocking pink or purple.

"Where's your girl friend?" I asked Cliff.

"Back home. I split up with her last week."

"Oh. I'm sorry."

He shrugged. "Nothing to be sorry about."

"It must be hard, though, if you really liked her."

Cliff was smiling at me in an indulgent way. "Yeah, I liked her," he said. The implication was: There are plenty more where she came from.

Just then Nelson came by. He clapped Cliff on the back. "Don't trust this guy," he said. "Don't trust him an inch farther than you can throw him."

I didn't think I could throw him anywhere, he was so big. I just smiled.

"So, how goes it, Cliff?" Nelson said.

"Pretty well," Cliff said. "It's a good party."

"Yeah, it is, isn't it? It's all Ali's doing. She arranged the whole thing. She's amazing, isn't she?"

"Sure," Cliff said. "As stepmothers go, I'd say she's pretty good."

"You would, huh?'

"Look, I don't *love* her. How could I? I don't even know her very well."

"So, Leslie loves me, and she doesn't know me that well."

Cliff looked at me. "You do?"

"Well . . ." The fact is, I don't even like Nelson that much, but in my champagny mood I smiled enigmatically. He's the kind of man you want to find you attractive, no matter what you think of him.

After a couple of dances Cliff wandered off, and I went back to Peter, who was still standing in the exact same place with the exact same expression. "Hi," I said.

"Hi," he said sourly.

"Look, Peter, you wouldn't dance with me, so I found someone who would. Is that so terrible?"

"You weren't just *dancing* with Cliff. I could see you. I happen to have excellent vision."

"He's not as bad as you said. I like him." I felt guilty in spite of myself.

"Great. You can write your name on his list of conquests."

"He said he broke up with that girl you told me about."

"So?"

"Well, I mean—"

"He probably has a line outside his door already."

"I don't even feel attracted to him if you want to know the truth," I lied.

"Listen, do what you want."

Suddenly I gave him a quick squeeze. "Peter, I like *you*, okay? Not him."

He looked embarrassed. "I know he's good-looking."

"That doesn't matter. Not to me."

But I could tell he wasn't convinced. Meanwhile the party kept getting smaller and smaller. Finally there was only us, Mom, Nelson, Cliff, and a few other people.

"I'm glad," Mom said. "Glad we did it, and glad it's over."

"Who's going to be next?" Nelson said. "How about you, Cliff?"

"Not me," Cliff said. "Peter, maybe."

"No way," Peter said.

"I don't think I'll get married till I'm thirty, at least," I said.

"A bunch of romantics," Nelson said. "You kids."

I wanted to show Peter my new room, but I felt funny doing it with everyone around. But then Mom asked if everyone would like to see the rest of the apartment. Peter followed along, his hands behind his back, like some old professor.

"Now, of course Leslie's room is a wreck," Mom said, "but—"

"It isn't!" I protested. I'd cleaned it up just that morning.

Mom just smiled. "It's a very convenient layout," she said. "See? She even has her own bathroom."

Peter glanced at me, but it was a kind of sly glance, as though he was thinking of us being together in that bed.

After Mom gave the tour, Cliff said, "Peter, we'd better hit the road. I promised Mom we'd get back tonight."

"Stay here," Mom said.

"No, we'd better go. Anyone need a lift? Leslie?"

"I live here!" I said.

"Oh, Christ, that's right. Just too much to drink, I guess."

After they'd gone, I helped Mom empty some ashtrays and pick things up, like dirty cups and plates. "I think they took it all right," she said.

"The party?"

"Our new arrangement. I mean, Peter and Cliff . . . I thought maybe they'd be mad because of Hope, but I think they understand."

For some reason I suddenly thought of Daddy and would have even called him on the phone, except it was two thirty in the morning.

"Les, get to bed. You look zonked."

"I am." I looked at Mom, who was as peppy as ever.

"Hey, Ali," Nelson called from their bedroom. "Finish cleaning up in the morning, okay?"

Mom padded off to their bedroom. It made me feel funny to think they would be making love. I guess that must be part of why they got married. Nelson is a sex object—no doubt about it. I don't know anything about what Mom and Daddy's sex life was like. There was a cool civility about the way they acted, but little physicality—no kisses or hugs, no sudden endearing gestures. I assumed that was just how people acted after twenty years of marriage.

I went into my room and got into my pajamas. Maybe someday I'll have fancy nightgowns, like Mom, but for now pajamas are just as good. I wonder if Peter will ever stay the whole night here. The thought of him, of how cold and distant he's been, gave me a pang. I want things to be good between us, the way they were over the summer when we could talk about everything. I hate the way it is now. God, I feel lonely.

Desperate Measures

"THIS IS WORSE THAN I THOUGHT," MOM SAID, STEPPING OFF the scale. "Now you, Peter."

It was the morning after the wedding. I stepped on the scale, not wanting to look, especially since I knew from the way my clothes fit that I'd gained. I looked down at it. "Shit," I said. It read one hundred and seventy-five, which is more than I've ever weighed.

"We've got to stay on our diets. If only we hadn't gained in the first place," Mom said. "It's all the fault of that damn machine."

On Mom's last birthday, Dad got her a Cuisinart. She hadn't used it much in the past, but this fall she'd begun cooking huge, delicious meals. She said she didn't see why we should eat in a fly-by-night manner, and besides, cooking was good therapy for her. I have to say this—she did cook some great things, but I guess they were fattening.

"Desperate measures are called for," Mom had finally said. "Maybe we should become vegetarians."

"We could jog," I said.

"That sounds so energetic," Mom said, sighing.

But she decided it was a good idea, and we both began getting up at six and jogging. Surprisingly, Mom was pretty good at it. It was me who got winded. She got a jogging suit and running shoes, but I did it in my regular shirt and jeans. It was hard getting out of bed and forcing myself to jog, but I did it. The trouble was, when we got home, I'd be starving and couldn't help eating a big breakfast.

"Traitor," she said the morning after the wedding. "You didn't even get up to jog with me this morning."

"Mom, come on," I said. "We didn't get home till two or something."

"I know," she said. "I heard you."

"How come? Were you still up?"

"No, I was kind of tossing around. I heard Cliff turn the damn radio on. What gets into him, wanting to listen to the radio at two in the morning?"

I shrugged. "He says its relaxing."

"It didn't bother you?"

"Uh-uh. I fell right to sleep."

We went down to the kitchen. I opened the refrigerator and got out a carton of Tropicana. I took a long gulp straight from the carton. It tasted good. I hadn't drunk that much at the party, but my mouth had a dry, powdery taste to it. "What're those?" I asked.

"College catalogs," Mom said. She was tossing all the big mail into one pile and the letters into another.

"What're they for?"

She made a face. "Planning my future supposedly. But I just can't decide."

"About what?"

"Well, remember Muriel Parsons?"

"Nope."

"You've met her, Peter. I used to live with her before I met Dad."

I couldn't remember. "Was she that one who came to visit last year, the one Dad said was so kooky?"

"That's just his thing. Muriel isn't really kooky, but her manner sometimes makes people uncomfortable. No, the point is, she runs a store in Chicago that sells children's toys and books, and I've been thinking maybe I could go there and help her out. I just think doing something would be good at this point, instead of moldering around. Also, I've decided to put the house on the market. Dad's right, it has too many bad memories."

"Yeah, but how about me?"

"I've been thinking of that. That's one of the things I'll have to consider."

"I mean, it's senior year and everything."

"Is that so important to you?"

"Not really."

She sighed. "Okay, well, it's just an idea. I'm also considering going back to school, in art history maybe. I thought one advantage to Chicago would be that Ken's there. It would be good to have some family around."

"Is that what you majored in? Art history?"

"Right." She sat looking at me with this funny expression. "Okay—out with it," she said.

"Out with what?"

"The wedding."

"Oh . . . the wedding. It was okay."

"Nope, sorry, that will not do. I want a blow by blow account."

I made a face. "Mom, come on. You know what weddings are like."

"How did Aline look? Gorgeous, huh?"

"Just regular," I said. "Like she always does."

"She couldn't have worn white . . . not for a second marriage."

"I guess not," I said. I started to take a couple of eggs out of the bin. "I'm going to make an omelet," I said.

"Peter, come on. What was she wearing?"

"I don't remember."

"You've got to. You saw her."

"I don't pay attention to things like that. But I think it wasn't white."

"Who was there?"

I took out the heavy saucepan that I use for omelets. When it comes to omelets, I'm pretty much of an expert. I learned how to make them when I was only six or seven. Even Dad, who doesn't like eggs much, says my omelets are the best he's ever tasted. I like making them as much as I like eating them. "Who was there?" I said, cracking the eggs. "Let me see. Well, for the wedding part it was just us and Leslie, but then they had this big party at their house."

"Were the Mattison's there?"

"It was just a big horde of people. I don't know your friends that well."

"The Mattisons are that couple who perform with those little theater groups. She's really tall with a pixie-type haircut, and he, well, he dresses in a kind of dandyish way, with vests and things, and he has sideburns."

I shook the pan around a little to let the eggs cook. I tried to remember. "Yeah, they were there," I said.

Mom sighed. "I bet everyone was there. I bet every last damn friend I had was there."

"There were quite a lot of people."

"Gloria was probably the only one who didn't go."

"Gloria who made that weaving thing in the living room?" I only remembered that because Dad always used to say it was the ugliest thing he ever saw. I know what he means—it looks like some old shaggy blanket that's just beginning to unravel. But Mom said people spend hundreds of dollars for Gloria's stuff.

"Gloria swore to me she wouldn't go even if they invited her. Maybe they didn't invite her."

I slid the omelet onto a plate. Then I took out the jam and dumped some on top of it. I felt really hungry.

"So you had a terrific time, huh?" Mom said.

"No," I said. "Who said that?"

"What'd you do, dance and that kind of thing?"

"I just kind of stood around." The omelet was great. I got up to get a glass of milk.

"I hope you danced with Leslie."

"Why should I have?"

"Well, she's such a—I feel so motherly when I see that girl. She always has such a bedraggled look to her."

"I don't think so."

"She always looks like she just lost her best friend. I like her, I don't mean that, but, well, maybe she's rebelling, but if she'd only stand up straight or something. . . . Did you?"

"I told you I didn't dance." I didn't feel like describing how Leslie had tried to make me do it. I sat down again. "She danced with Cliff a lot."

"Where is he anyway? It's— Look at that, it's past one! Peter, go upstairs and throw some cold water on him, will you?"

"He said he felt like catching up on his sleep."

"Did he say anything about Margy?"

"Just . . . I guess he had sort of a rough time with her. She's been really depressed, and he said he had to sit up with her nights, looking after her."

Mom squinted thoughtfully. "I wish we'd at least met her. . . . I don't see why both he and Ken had to go so far away to college."

Actually I'd thought of applying to Stanford, which is no closer than Berkeley or Chicago, but last spring I decided to try for early admission to Harvard. That way, if they take you, your worries are over by December. "I guess they just thought those were the best places."

"No," Mom said. "I don't kid myself. They wanted out. Why not? I want out myself." She began leafing through a catalog.

While she did, I thought about the wedding party. Why

had I acted like such a jerk? I was hoping that it would be an opportunity for Leslie and me to get back together again, but it seemed like all she wanted to do was flirt with everyone in sight. She had to have known that dancing the night away with Cliff would get to me; she's not *that* insensitive. I don't understand her at times. It's true, I probably should have come into the city more after the summer, but Mom seemed to feel so betrayed and lonely that I hated leaving her by herself, and I felt if she knew I was going in to see Leslie, it would add insult to injury, as though I'd gone over to the enemy, as it were. I'm not good on the phone—I never know what to say. Once I sat down and wrote Leslie a long letter about how I felt, but when I reread it, it sounded stupid and sentimental, so I ripped it up and threw it away.

Maybe she's met someone in the city and is ashamed to tell me. Maybe all she was after was a quickie way to lose her virginity. Over the summer I'd felt there was really something going between us. It seemed real on both sides. Now I wonder if I didn't just let my imagination run away with me. I'm certainly going to try and cool it whenever I see her from now on.

I glanced over at Mom, who had closed the catalog. "Well, one thing I know," she said. "I am *never* getting married again. If I ever try to, tie me up in chains and sit on me, will you?"

"Okay."

"Gloria says her life really began after her divorce. She says being on her own is the best thing that ever happened to her."

"You'll be okay, Mom." Since we'd gotten back from Fire Island, we'd had a lot of these conversations. Sometimes I get the feeling Mom says things to me that she'd usually say to a friend, and I don't know how to respond.

I went upstairs to get dressed. Cliff was already in the bathroom. He yawned and stretched when he saw me. "Hi, Pete. How's it going?"

"Pretty good."

"What time is it, anyway?"

"One something."

"Come on down with me while I have breakfast."

"I have this test in history. I should go to the library."

"You can go later. It's open till five, isn't it?"

Cliff never studied hard in high school, and he still managed to get into pretty good colleges, but I'm not like that. Even though I know senior year grades don't count that much and I have a pretty good crack at Harvard, I still study just as hard as ever. Compulsion, I guess. It's an escape and always has been, a world I excel in, where only my mind counts, not my lumbering, idiot body.

Mom was just heading out the door when Cliff and I came down to the kitchen. "Hail!" she said to Cliff. "You must be an apparition."

"I'm a growing boy, and I need my sleep," Cliff said.

"I've heard that one before. Hey, don't keep Peter from going to the library. He needs to do some studying."

Cliff winked at me. "Me prevent him from doing his studying?"

"I did some of it last week, Mom. I really did. Now I have to organize what I did." That was only half-true, but she seemed to accept it. I think my getting into Harvard means a lot to Mom.

When she had left, Cliff stretched. "God, I had an incredible dream about Margy." He grinned.

"I thought you broke up with her."

"Yeah, but we still make it together occasionally, out of sheer horniness or nostalgia or whatever. I really dig her, I just don't want to get tied down this early in the game. Look at Mom and Dad. Maybe if they'd waited longer, they would've realized they were totally unsuited to each other."

I got down a box of cereal. "What's so unsuited about them? I always thought they seemed to get along pretty well."

Cliff shrugged. "I think Dad needs someone a little more . . . lively. I mean, Mom's great, but, let's face it, she's over forty, and her figure's shot. Dad's more like me. He needs variety."

I poured some milk on top of the cereal. "Leslie's mother's forty."

"Yeah, but she's a lot younger looking. And she works; she's out in the world. I always got the feeling Mom was just hanging around waiting for Dad to come home. That kind of thing can bring a man down. Believe me, I know."

"How do you know?" I said irritably. "How many times have you been married?"

Cliff laughed. "Look, you don't have to be married for girls to get that way. Margy was that way already, even though I never breathed a word about marriage. Like, Monday, Wednesday, and Friday I had chem lab, which ended at four. But sometimes I'd go for a walk or out for a beer. So I'd get back to my room, and she'd be there saying, 'Where were you? I was worried. I thought you'd been in an accident.' It really got to me. Mom can be a little like that, clinging."

"I don't think Dad's such a prize," I said, eating my cereal. I was conscious that Cliff, who isn't a pound overweight, was just sitting there with a glass of juice and some vitamins.

"He's a good-looking guy, he keeps in shape. I think women go for him, probably always will."

"So you think this won't last? He'll have other girl friends?" I couldn't believe that he'd go through a whole divorce and remarriage and then start all over again!

"As long as she doesn't catch him, what's to worry? He'll be careful. But sure, maybe they'll make it. I think he was opting for a whole other life-style, something a little flashier than life out here. Mom was suited to raising kids, this old house, but she doesn't fit into the way his life is now."

I realized I'd finished the whole bowl of cereal. I'd

forgotten I had already had an omelet. "You're really cynical," I said, hating myself for being such a glutton.

"Yeah?" He looked surprised. "Anyway, we got a cute little stepsister out of the deal."

My stomach tightened. "Who, Leslie?"

"Yeah, I like her. She's a nice dancer. You can tell quite a lot about girls after a couple of dances, how they'd be—"

I got up and walked out of the room. I didn't feel like listening to the rest. God, I'm glad he's away at college. I really despise him at times. Leslie's lucky to be an only child.

After Cliff left, life settled back into its normal pattern. But it was true—the house did seem huge for just Mom and me. It was four bedrooms, a giant den with a bar in the basement, a library. I gather it was pretty big when they bought it fifteen years ago, but then they added on an extra room and enlarged the kitchen. When all of us were at home, we used to eat in the dining room. It isn't that fancy a room, but it has a long table in the middle and stiff-backed chairs all around. When Ken and Cliff left for college, Mom took a leaf out of the table to make it smaller. She, Dad, and I would all sit at one end. But after Dad left, it seemed ridiculous for just the two of us to sit there, so we took to eating in the kitchen.

The other thing is that before this we had a housekeeper, Bertha, who did the cooking. She was a superb cook. She claimed she hated to cook, but whatever Mom asked her to fix, plain or fancy, she did a terrific job. Now she just comes in twice a week to clean, and Mom's taken over the cooking. Plus, she's put both of us on viciously severe diets. Everything gets weighed. Supposedly we can't have more than three or four ounces of meat or even fish as a main course. She trims off all the fat. No potatoes or rice, just steamed vegetables. God, I hate healthy things! At night I have obscene dreams about falling into vats of brownie batter. Plus I cheat a lot. I never mean to, but sometimes I wake up in the middle of the night and can't get back to sleep. I know if I don't sleep, I'll be a zombie at school, so I allow myself to have a small snack. The trouble is, sometimes I spy some leftover piece of cheese or coffee cake and wolf it down before I even know what I'm doing. Since I don't want Mom to know, I try and just eat dry cereal out of the box or nuts or someting she won't notice is missing. Actually I think she may cheat too because neither of us has lost a pound so far.

"I was terrible today," Mom confessed at dinner one night. It was about a month after the wedding, in early November. "I passed a bakery that sells croissants, and I bought one and ate it in three bites. I feel so ashamed! No wonder I lost a husband! I have *no* willpower! I'm a disgrace. And I've passed it all on to you."

"Mom, it's not hereditary," I said. "If you eat less, you lose."

Mom speared an asparagus gloomily. "It *is*! It's like one of those Ibsen plays where the sins of the father are visited on the children. Ken and Cliff are just like Nelson. You couldn't make them fat if you *tried*, if you *forced* food down their throats. They love sports, they're active, lean, healthy people, and they'll probably live to be two hundred—and if they weren't my own sons, I'd hate them."

"I cheat a lot too," I said. "I get up at night and have snacks."

Mom laughed. "I know. One night I woke up, and the first thought I had was about that piece of coffee cake left over from breakfast. I raced downstairs and it was gone. . . . But, Peter, seriously, it's worse for you. You're young! You've got to do something. If you look like this when you go for your college interviews, what'll they think?"

"Mom, come on. They care about my grades and my SATs, not my weight."

She shook her head. "No, they want people who are well rounded." Then, realizing her slip, she gave a hoot of nervous laughter. "I mean, they want—what is that phrase?—a healthy mind and a healthy body. And how about your social life?"

I turned red. "*You* got married," I said evenly, reaching for a roll.

"Yeah, but you want to know how? When I met Nelson, I'd just had pneumonia, and I'd lost fifteen pounds. He thought that was the way I normally looked, and I was so petrified of losing him, I literally lost my appetite. The only time in my life that ever happened." She smiled wryly. "I wish that feeling would come back."

"Maybe you'll meet some new guy and you'll lose it again," I suggested. "Maybe you'll get pneumonia again."

"A new guy." Mom sighed. "You know what the statistics are for women my age? Even thin ones? No, this is a new era of life. I did marriage. I did kids. And you know, I always said when I was younger that I had three goals in life: to have a happy marriage, to have terrific kids I'd be proud of, and to find work I could enjoy. Well, I did one and a half of those things. That's not so bad, is it?"

"Why one and a half?" I asked.

"Well, *I* was happy . . . and I was half of our marriage." Suddenly her face crumpled.

I got out of my chair and patted her on the shoulder. "Mom, I'll lose weight," I said. "You'll be proud of me too."

Mom sniffed. "I am proud of you already, Peter. Who cares what you weigh? That's all superficial. Let's throw out the scale! When you meet a girl you like, you'll lose just like that, overnight. Take my word for it."

I smiled weakly.

With Compelling Ardor

NINETY-NINE FOUR ISN'T A FEVER," MIRA SAID. "GET TO school tomorrow, or you might as well forget the whole thing."

I panicked. Every month practically, when I get my period, I get a low-grade fever which the doctor says he can't really explain *or* cure. If it's accompanied by bad cramps, I take the day off. This week we had auditions for the senior play, and I'd been out the day before. We were doing *The Barretts of Wimpole Street*. It's by someone named Rudolf Besier. Because our school is all girls, we put plays on with the boys' school across the campus, the Windsor School for Boys. (Ours is the Windsor School for Girls.) For years there's been talk of merging the two schools, but even if it eventually happens, it won't affect my life at all since it's my senior year.

There are two major reasons I want desperately to get the lead in *The Barretts of Wimpole Street*. The first is that playing Elizabeth Barrett Browning is a dream of mine. I used to write poetry, especially in my first two years of high school. It's not immortal stuff. In fact, some of it's pretty crummy, but I love writing it, and my English teacher, Mr. Speer, said a few poems were so good I should submit them to a national contest. I didn't win, but after Mr. Speer read the ones that did, he said that he thought mine were much better. So you can see why I feel this is a perfect part for me. I even look like Elizabeth Barrett Browning. I'm thin, and I have really pale skin and black hair. Any guy that's ever remotely liked me has said I'm sensitive or artistic-looking. Maybe that's just a compliment for them to toss at a girl who doesn't have big boobs, but actually there's some truth in it. The only problem is I feel strange about some of Elizabeth's lines. There are really corny ones like:

> Yes, Robert, but what have I to give you? I have so little of all that love asks for. I have no beauty and no health—and I'm no longer young.

Most of the lines have cues in parentheses after them: "(with restrained spiritual ecstasy)" or "(with compelling ardor)."

Compelling ardor. Okay, here comes the dopey reason that I want to play Elizabeth so much. It's that the guy who'll probably play Robert Browning is Vladimir Ascher, who's six feet two and has coal-black eyes that could bore a hole straight through to Moscow (his parents came here when he was six). Without his looks, he might not get the part. But face it, even Ms. Brandemour, our drama teacher, who believes in casting people counter to type, is not going to give Robert Browning to Mel Friedman, who is great at character parts but only five feet two, or Gil Mendoza, who is probably the best actor at Windsor but has acne that even stage makeup barely conceals. I'm not even the type who goes for hulks, but since Peter has vanished from my life, playing passionate love scenes opposite Vladimir could be one of the few things that will redeem this year.

* * *

"I'm so pleased to see you, dear," Brandemour said the next day when I showed up for auditions. "We needed you yesterday."

I tried not to smile but felt a lot better. I still had cramps, but I'd taken a Motrin. "I had a chance to reread the play," I said.

"Well," Brandemour said. "What I'd like to do today is run through a few of the same scenes with different people in different parts. Mel, how about trying Captain Surtees Cook, and Leslie, dear, since you were out yesterday, you take Henrietta. We'll try the scene where they come to visit Elizabeth. Bryna, you play Elizabeth."

My heart sank at Brandemour just assuming Bryna Hissler would do Elizabeth. Why had she stuck me with Henrietta? It didn't make sense when I wanted to play Elizabeth so badly and the five other girls who were auditioning all wanted Henrietta's part. She's the younger sister, pretty, vivacious, rebellious, who's supposedly having a clandestine affair with a military officer. Mira would be perfect for the part, but she's decided to learn lighting. "But Ms. Brandemour, I don't think I'd be right for Henrietta," I said, stuttering slightly.

You're never, ever supposed to say that, but I'd practically memorized all of Elizabeth's lines. And Henrietta is about as unlike me as anyone in the whole damn play, except maybe Arabella, the adorable cousin who always talks in baby talk and tries to seduce the father.

"Why don't you let *me* be the judge of that?" Brandemour said, smiling firmly. "And don't worry, you'll have a chance at other parts."

What could I say? I did the scene. In it I show off my boyfriend, Captain Cook—Mel Friedman—to Elizabeth. Henrietta is the kind of girl I'd hate if I met her, a total flirt, impish, teasing. According to the stage notes I was supposed to get down on my knees and buckle on Captain

Cook's sword. Since we didn't have props, I thought I'd skip that, but Brandemour called out, "Just pantomime, dear. Remember, it's a *heavy* sword. Kneel in front of him, arms around his waist. The whole effectiveness of the scene is that your father catches you in the act, as it were."

I know Brandemour isn't a sadist, but Christ, it really looked like we were about to have oral sex. She made me repeat that about three times. When the father, who was played by Gil, walked in, I was so relieved I gave out a cry.

Brandemour looked pleased. "Very nice, *very* nice. Any expression of love is totally forbidden in this house, you see, and Henrietta is the only one with the courage to openly rebel against her father's prohibitions."

"How about Elizabeth?" I said.

"She does it secretly," Brandemour said. "She's a very inward, repressed person. That was nice, the interaction between you and Bryna. You're very close, though you're such different people, or should I say because of that? All right, let's try an Elizabeth Browning scene, shall we? I think the one where he convinces her to run away with him. Vladimir? Bryna?"

I slunk back to my seat. Mira sat next to me. "You were good," she said cheerfully.

"I don't *want* that part," I hissed, very softly so no one but Mira would hear.

I tried to watch Bryna and Vladimir do their scene just to see how she was playing it and what I could do differently. They look almost like twins. They're both very tall, with thick black hair and heavy eyebrows. When Bryna read lines like "I love you too well to let you waste your manhood pursuing the pale ghost of a woman," it seemed like a joke. Vladimir was stiff. He "enunciates" lines, almost puffing out his chest. I thought they didn't play well together, but when they were done, Brandemour said, "*Much* better, Vladimir. You have to realize Robert Browning is a bit of a jerk."

Vladimir looked taken aback. "I thought he was the big romantic lead."

"He *thinks* he is. There's a difference. Really he's mainly in love with himself."

"Poor Elizabeth," Bryna said mockingly.

"Yes," Brandemour went on, chain-lighting a cigarillo. "But Elizabeth knows him inside out, far better than he knows himself. Women *always* know men far better than men know themselves. That's our tragedy." She laughed hoarsely.

Vladimir looked hurt. "I think that's a prejudice, Ms. Brandemour."

"Do you, Vladimir? Well, we are all entitled to our prejudices, you to yours and me to mine. That's what makes the world go 'round."

We spent all afternoon going over different scenes. Once I was Arabella, and Vladimir played the father. I had to sit on his knee and fiddle with his supposed beard while he said things like "You're a distractingly lovely little creature." I was petrified that Brandemour would like me in the part and tried to hold back, but she kept yelling, "Pour it on *thick*, Leslie! Remember, this woman would try to seduce a lamppost if it suited her purposes. That's right. Look deep into his eyes. You love the fact that he's this uptight, fearsome widower. You know you could reduce him to a bowl of jelly in one *second* in bed."

I don't know who turned redder at that, me or Vladimir. I couldn't reduce anyone in bed to a bowl of anything. That's Brandemour's style, just like her slouchy Garbo-style hats and being intense and outspoken, but it can be horribly embarrassing.

What bothered me the most was that I never got to play Elizabeth opposite Vladimir at all. I had my big scene, quote unquote, opposite Gil. Basically I think Gil's a better actor than Vladimir, but you'd have to have a sack over your head to think of him as an intense, romantic hero.

When he grabbed me and started exclaiming about how much he loved me, I had to use real willpower not to back away.

"That's right, dear," Brandemour shouted. "*Some* resistance . . . but not *too* much. Remember, for all your protests, you'd be out the door with this man in no time at all were it not for your sick relationship with your father. What do you think you were fantasizing about all these years when you were writing poem after ghastly poem?"

"Her poems weren't ghastly," I said, horrified. "She's a great poet!"

"Nonsense," Brandemour fired back. "Elizabeth and Robert were perfectly suited to each other. Neither of them wrote a decent line in their lives. He was all pretense, and she was all romantic slosh."

"But then what's the point of the play?" Gil asked. "I thought this was the great romance of the nineteenth century."

"It is!" Brandemour said. She leaped on the stage in her faded jeans and man's jacket. "Who says great poets are better lovers than rotten poets? What makes this play wonderful is the intensity of these people's feelings. Elizabeth B., caught between two blind, headstrong men, father and lover, trying to find a way to live her own life. It's a *very* modern situation."

"Do you think she's a feminist?" I asked tentatively.

Brandemour stamped out her cigarillo. "God knows. Sure, let's call her a feminist if that'll make all you girls identify with her more. To me those definitions aren't worth beans."

"I think *he's* a feminist," Mel said seriously. "Because he loves her for her poetry, not for her, you know. . . ."

"Were they happy once they ran off together?" Bryna asked wistfully.

Brandemour sighed. "Let's hope so, dear. Luckily that's beyond the scope of our play. But let's assume that they were, and that they did more than write those godawful immortal sonnets."

After school Mira and I went out for a snack at the Ramble, a delicatessen near school. "So what do you think?" I asked. "Was I good?"

Mira nodded. "You were . . . but why'd she have you read opposite *Gil*?"

"Search me."

"I mean, there's casting against type, and there's casting against type. If he played Robert, the audience would walk out after one scene!"

I laughed gloomily. "How did you think Bryna was today? As Elizabeth, I mean?"

"Well, for a supposed invalid, she's pretty vigorous—she looks like she could arm wrestle him to the ground."

"I know! Only Brandemour says that's the point, that she *is* really strong. She's just masquerading as weak for some neurotic reason. It's over her mother's death or something."

Mira spooned up some whipped cream from her hot chocolate. "You looked cute on Vladimir's lap, L."

"Yeah, I now have fantasy material for the next two years," I admitted. "But if she gives me Arabella, I'll *kill* her." I bit into my Danish, which was half-stale.

"Stranger things have happened," Mira said.

"I just won't be in the play," I whimpered. "There's a limit, and talking baby talk to men is it."

She grinned. "How about sitting on Vlad's lap? That didn't make up for it?"

My voice rose to a squeak, I was so excited. "He won't *be* the father! If he was, it'd be different."

All night I dreamed about the play, being in it, not being in it, it really happening. I felt like I didn't sleep much, but I think I probably did. All morning I only half-concentrated on classes because it's at lunch hour that Brandemour posts the cast lists. Mira had promised me she wouldn't go and look before I did. I wanted to get there fast so I wouldn't run into anyone else, but as I came down the stairs, I saw Bryna walking away in the other direction. Her back was to me, and I tried to interpret whether she'd gotten Elizabeth by the slump of her shoulders, but I couldn't. At least she wasn't turning cartwheels down the hall. I crossed my fingers once tight, prayed briefly, and walked over.

I was Henrietta.

After I'd stared at the list for a moment—Bryna was Elizabeth, Vladimir was Robert, Mel was Captain Cook, Gil was the father—I slunk away. If only it were the last period! I just couldn't see sitting through classes, especially with Bryna in almost all of them. I decided, though I've almost never done this, to cut the rest of school. I started upstairs for my locker, hoping I wouldn't even run into Mira, who was in the lunchroom, waiting for me. Then I passed the auditorium and saw Brandemour sitting at the back, reading, her feet up on the next chair. On impulse I pushed the heavy door open.

"Ms. Brandemour?"

She looked down, then put down her papers. "I think you're going to be a sensational Henrietta," she exclaimed.

"I—I don't see why," I stammered. "I'm not right for the part. She's everything I'm *not*! I'm *not* vivacious or rebellious. I would have been perfect for Elizabeth. It isn't fair!" I sounded like I was going to cry.

Brandemour looked at me sympathetically but with that slight air of detachment she always has. "I think there are things in you, Leslie, that you're not totally aware of. When you played that scene where you defy your father, there was a lot of inner fire and passion that sparked right off the stage. It was very compelling."

I couldn't look at her. "I think Bryna's a good actress," I said, "but she's so . . . large. That's not the way Elizabeth is supposed to be. She's fragile and delicate. Bryna will look ridiculous."

"I thought of that," Brandemour said thoughtfully, "but

looks aren't *that* crucial. You see, for one thing, Elizabeth spends most of the play sitting, so Bryna's height won't be as evident as it might be. And Bryna has a kind of awesome heaviness, a sense of *deep* misery. I'm not trying to do psychodrama, but I happen to know she and her father have and *exceptionally* difficult relationship. I could sense she was drawing on that, and I found it very moving. . . . Yes, you could have played Elizabeth and very nicely too, dear, but who could have played Henrietta? She's a key part, you know."

"Alice! Nancy! Dorie! They all wanted to be Henrietta," I cried, exasperated.

"For all the wrong reasons," Brandemour said crisply. "Most people have a very faulty and skin-deep notion of who they are and what they're capable of. Trust me, dear. Playing Henrietta will be good for you. A real breakthrough."

I went home. Mom and Nelson both work till almost six, so the house was empty. I felt shitty. I wanted so much to be Elizabeth! And I know, I just *know* I would've done a good job. Even if Vladimir wasn't Robert. So Byrna has a difficult relationship with her father! What difference does *that* make. Brandemour's productions are good, but I think they *are* psychodramas in a way.

At dinner Mom asked, "So how's the great poetess?" She knew I'd been reading *The Barretts* for the past couple of weeks.

"Bryna Hissler is playing Elizabeth," I said flatly. "I'm Henrietta."

"Which one is she?" Mom asked. "I don't recall."

"One of the sisters."

"Well, they always say it's more of a test of your acting if you don't get the lead," Nelson said, refilling his wineglass.

"But Leslie would have been perfect as Elizabeth," Mom said indignantly. "What was Ms. Brandemour thinking of? Bryna Hissler is a female hulk. She looks like she could sling Browning over her shoulder and carry him to Italy on her back."

I tried to laugh. "Yeah, well . . . I had the lead last year. She wanted to make it fair."

"You'll be terrific," Nelson said. "Just concentrate on making Henrietta the center of the play, and she will be."

"I'll try." I looked at him and suddenly hated him—for not being Daddy, for wrecking their marriage, for being so fuckingly self-satisfied and handsome.

Despite my feelings about Nelson, and a kind of inner pain about Peter, things have actually gone fairly smoothly in the six weeks since the wedding. Mom is happy and is nice to me; she seems more interested than usual in my life, but in a good, not an intrusive way. She and Nelson are out a lot in the evening, and I feel lonely then. I do see Daddy often, two or three times a week, but it's not the same. I feel like a visitor in my own home. All my old furniture is still there, but it looks strange to me. And yet I don't feel comfortable in the new apartment either, where everything is so glossy and elegant. Nelson is clearly trying to be a good stepfather, but I don't think he knows how. He only knows how to flirt with women, and he does it with me, probably not even consciously. Sometimes it makes me nervous: I worry Mom will mind.

The night of the casting she had to go out after dinner to meet a friend. I was in my room doing my homework when Nelson looked in. "Leslie, I wondered if I could . . . We haven't had a chance to talk that much since Aline and I . . ."

"About what?" I hope I didn't sound as hostile as I felt.

"Well, I guess I primarily wanted to say how delighted I am to have a daughter after all these years. I always wanted one and kept wishing each time Hope gave birth. So it's a little as though, belatedly, my wishes have been granted."

I'm not your daughter, I thought, but I didn't say anything.

"Of course, I'm your stepfather, not your real father," he went on. "I realize that. I'm not trying to take Preston's place or even . . . It's just a nice change having a lovely young woman at the table instead of three loud, obese sons."

By "obese" I guess he meant Peter since Cliff and Ken certainly aren't that heavy. "I'm not a lovely young woman," I said coolly, meaning, treat me as a step-daughter, not a woman.

But Nelson seemed to take my remark to mean I wasn't confident about my appearance. He bent down to ruffle my hair. "Yes, you are. And your self-doubt just makes you more appealing. I can assure you that once you get to college, many young men will find you extremely desirable."

I shrugged and laughed. "Let's hope!"

"It's a certainty. And I envy every one of them." With that he left the room.

I tried, once I was alone, to wonder how I'd feel about Nelson if he weren't married to Mom, if he were one of my teachers or the father of a friend. I think I'd still think he was a phony, but it's true, the more extreme angry feelings I have are because of our circumstances, his cheating on Peter's mother, his belittling Peter, his sexist garbage about young women.

Suddenly I wanted so much to talk to Peter. It seemed awful that this breach had arisen between us when he was the only one who could really understand how I felt. Anxiously I reached for the phone and dialed his number. My hands were icy cold.

"Oh, hi," he said, sounding a little stiff. "How goes it?"

I decided not to say anything about our not having seen each other in so long, not since the wedding, actually. Instead I told him about the play and not getting Elizabeth.

"Well, won't it be more interesting playing someone who's *not* like you?" he said in his mild Peter-like way. "I mean, I've never been in a play and never will, so I don't really know, but—"

"No, it won't," I snapped. "I have to go around buckling on some person's sword and dancing the polka all around the stage! I'm going to be *rotten!* I'll make a total ass of myself."

"Well, anyhow, you'll graduate right after and won't even see those people again, so what does it matter?" Peter said.

Suddenly I felt like a fool for calling him. Not because I really think the boy should always make the first move, but because he sounded so detached, so unjoyful about hearing from me.

"So what have you been doing? Anything special?" I said.

"No, nothing much. I had my Harvard interview."

"How'd it go?"

"Okay. I'm trying for early admission, so I should hear pretty soon. Dad went there, which ought to help."

He'd told me all that over the summer. Has he had amnesia? I didn't know what to say. I decided to give it one last try. "Listen, do you want to come into the city this weekend?" I said. "I'm going to the Metropolitan Museum with Daddy. You could join us."

"Do you want me to?"

"No—that's why I'm asking you."

"I thought you might want to be alone with your father, that's all," Peter said in a distant way.

"I see him twice a week."

"Sure, I don't see why not," Peter said.

"Well, don't do me any favors!"

"Les, I *want* to come."

We arranged a place to meet in the museum, and he said he'd be there promptly at two on Saturday. I wondered if I'd been a jerk to call him.

Serenity and Earthiness

I GOT TO THE MET LATE, AT ALMOST TWO TWENTY. I RACED up the steps and loped down the corridor to the exhibition of Dutch paintings. From across the room I saw Leslie and her father, arm in arm, their backs to me, looking at a painting of some huge feast. Leslie and her father are both small, and arm in arm like that, they looked almost like a couple, or at least you sensed the closeness between them. I wished, if I was going to come all the way into the city, I could have just met her alone.

When she'd called, I'd felt a little guilty that I hadn't been the one to check in with her and see how she was doing. But every excuse I'd thought of for calling had seemed inane. I assume she called because she wanted to get back in touch, but she sounded so impatient and unwarm, like the call was almost more of a duty, not really wanting to hear how I was. She hardly asked me anything about myself, just went on and on about the play she was going to be in. When I mentioned applying for early admission to Harvard, she didn't even *say* anything! Not that I wanted her to gasp in amazement at how bright I am, but it was almost like she didn't hear me. Frankly I don't even know why she ended up asking me to come into the city. Duty again?

Just then Leslie's father saw me and waved.

"Sorry I'm late," I said. I saw Leslie look at me and then try to repress what was clearly an expression of disgust, probably at how much weight I'd gained. Suddenly I felt ugly and slovenly, and wished I hadn't come at all. Of course her father is plump, but he's in his fifties, and it doesn't seem to matter that much with men his age.

"How do you like this lovely young lady?" Leslie's father said.

I thought at first he meant Leslie, but he was pointing to a painting of a girl eating oysters by someone named Jan Steen. "It's good," I said. I never know what to say about paintings, whether I like them or not.

"Look at that marvelous sly, avaricious expression on her face." He smiled. "She'll eat all those oysters, every last one, if they don't catch her in time."

I know he was just commenting on the painting, but I felt as though it was somehow directed at me.

"I hate oysters," Leslie said, shuddering. She still held her father's arm. "They're so slimy."

We moved on to another painting. It showed a couple getting married. They both looked stiff and uncomfortable and had big white ruffs around their necks.

"It's funny," Leslie said, moving closer to the painting. "She looks pregnant, doesn't she? Is she supposed to be?" She glanced at me.

"I think that's just the way they dressed," I said.

"They don't look very happy about getting married,"

Leslie went on, looking back at the painting. "They look more like they're going to a funeral."

"I think it's the ruffs," Leslie's father said. "Once they get those off and relax, have a few flagons of mulled wine, they'll feel a whole lot better." He raised his hands in a toast. "Cheer up, good people," he addressed the couple. "If you think you feel bad now—"

Leslie's father started holding forth on the painters of the seventeenth century, why one painter was better than another. He's a smart guy, but Leslie listened to everything he said with a wide-eyed, intent expression which irritated the hell out of me.

We stopped in front of a painting of a couple sitting at a table. "You know what I love about the Dutch is their combination of serenity and earthiness," Leslie's father said. "Look at those two dogs copulating in the corner! A perfect touch. At first you don't even notice it."

Leslie frowned and stared at the dogs. "Is that what they're doing?" she said, flustered. "I thought they were just . . . playing."

It was pretty obvious that they weren't playing. I wondered why Leslie's father had called attention to it. "I guess it's a kind of playing," I said, smiling, but Leslie wouldn't look at me. *Hey, kid, we did some playing once, remember?*

"It's a part of life," Leslie's father said, "a perfectly natural part, and yet other painters might not have thought it worthy of inclusion. But how much poorer a painting it would be without that!"

We all stared at the copulating dogs, thinking our individual thoughts, until Leslie's father moved into the next room. The first painting there was of two giant sea tortoises face to face. "Oh, look, aren't they sweet?" Leslie said. "They look so friendly, like they're best friends."

"You know, Holland had recently discovered the New

World," Leslie's father said. "These may have been the first such beasts that any Dutchman had ever seen."

"Or any Dutch woman," Leslie put in.

He laughed. "Any Dutch *person*." To me he added, "I have to watch my *p*'s and *q*'s around this girl. Is she that strict with you, Peter?"

"Sometimes," I said, looking at Leslie, who turned away. She was acting like I was an intruder, some person they'd happened to bump into and couldn't shake off. Fuck her. Who called who? I didn't get it.

After the Dutch paintings Leslie's father wanted to see a show of anatomical drawings by Leonardo da Vinci. They were mainly small black and white sketches of bones, hands, legs, muscles.

"Ugh, I hate these," Leslie said. "They're so mechanical."

"They were very important in the history of anatomy," her father said. "Leonardo was one of the first to actually study the human body from a scientific point of view."

"The thorax of an ox!" she said and without another word raced out, leaving me with her father.

We went through the rest of the show together. He didn't act any differently now that Leslie had disappeared. In fact, he didn't even refer to it. "How's your mother, Peter?" he asked.

"She's okay. She's trying to decide what to do about her future."

"Yes, she mentioned that last summer."

"She might even move to Chicago to live with a friend once I'm out of school."

"A fresh start might be wise," he said, "after all this unpleasantness." You would have thought the "unpleasantness" had nothing to do with him.

"Sure, I think it's a good idea," I said.

When we came out of the show, Leslie was sitting on a

bench near where they sold postcards, just gazing off into space. "Well, I guess I'll be heading back," I said as we were getting our coats.

"So soon?" Leslie's father said. "I thought you'd both come back to my apartment and have a quick bite to eat. Or is your mother expecting you?"

Actually Mom wasn't expecting me back for dinner. I hesitated. I looked at Leslie, waiting for her to say something about wanting me to stay.

"It's so stupid to come in just for an hour," she said impatiently. "What's so important that you have to go straight back?"

"Nothing." I stared at her coldly.

"Well, *we're* going to have dinner," she said, "but if you don't want to stay, don't! We're not going to get down on our hands and knees and beg you!"

I laughed. "Hey, I didn't expect you to."

"We could order up some Chinese food," Leslie's father said smoothly. "Do you like Chinese food, Peter?" He acted as if it'd been agreed that I'd stay.

Leslie's father's apartment, the one he used to live in with her mother, isn't that big. There're two bedrooms, and Leslie's was still the way it would have been if she still lived there. I wondered what stuff she'd taken to the new apartment. I stood in the doorway of her room. A minute later she came back and said her father was going out to get the food from a place on the corner.

"I like this room better than the new one," she said. "It's like this is my *real* room, and the other one—I don't know."

There was a moment of silence.

"I get the feeling you wish I hadn't come in," I blurted out.

"Why would I have asked you to, then?"

"I don't now. Why *did* you?"

She looked all around the room. "I guess I just can't

figure out what kind of relationship we're going to have now," she said in a much softer tone. "Technically we're stepbrother and stepsister, but—"

"That doesn't mean anything."

"Yes, it does!"

"If you want to use it as an excuse to make everything the way it was before the summer, okay. But it's just an excuse."

"It's not, Peter! We *are* stepbrother and stepsister."

"Leslie, cut it out, okay? We're anything we want to be."

She turned away. "I guess I don't *know* what I want."

I hesitated. "I'm sorry I got fat again."

I was hoping she'd say, "Oh, I didn't even notice," but she just said, "Why did you?"

"I don't know. I like to eat." God, I hate her sometimes!

She looked puzzled. "Don't you have any willpower?"

"No."

Leslie's expression softened. "Peter, I just . . . I think maybe anyway it'd be better to . . . Let's just be stepbrother and stepsister. We can talk, be close. The other way it would be so complicated and crazy almost. And it's going to be a tough year for both of us with college and all."

The fact is, I half-agreed with what she was saying, but I still felt hurt and angry and wished it had been something we'd arrived at independently. This way it came across as an excuse for her not to have anything to do with me physically. I caught sight of myself in the mirror on her closet door and felt a stab of disgust.

"You'll lose eventually," Leslie said uncertainly. "Nelson said he was going to play squash with you. That burns up a lot of calories."

"Your father's fat," I pointed out.

Leslie smiled indulgently. "I know, poor Daddy. He's so

hopelessly sedentary." But she said it with such love and devotion that it came out sounding like a compliment.

"I guess at his age it doesn't matter," I said.

"Maybe he'll want to remarry eventually. He's such a sweetie. I would think millions of women would want to marry him."

We heard the door slam, and Leslie's father called to us from the next room that the food had arrived. We ate in the living room, putting out plates on the coffee table. Leslie's father had bought a ton of stuff, about five different main courses, soup, and rice. "This isn't real food," he said, "delicious as it is. It's all vegetables really."

"Peter's trying to lose weight, Daddy," Leslie said. "You shouldn't have gotten so much."

Leslie's father looked at me in surprise. "Well, Chinese food won't hurt him. He just needs a little exercise, that's all."

"I hate exercise," I said, reaching for the barbecued spareribs.

"So do I," Leslie's father said. "Thank heaven I'm beyond all that absurd and fruitless vanity about my appearance. And thank heaven not all women are so preoccupied with surface."

Leslie was lying on the floor, propped up with a pillow. She was wearing a red skirt and red tights and a black turtleneck which outlined her figure pretty directly. I tried not to start fantasizing. *We're stepbrother and stepsister, and anyway, she's a jerk, and her breasts are too small, and who needs her?*

"Do you think Elizabeth Barrett Browning was a feminist?" Leslie asked her father.

"In what sense, sweetheart?"

"Well, she changed her name to Browning."

"Everyone did then," he said. "What does it matter? She was an interesting and inspiring person. It took courage to do what she did, to break away from her father, to run off with Browning."

Leslie flung down her fork. "Why didn't she make *me* Elizabeth? I would have been so good! I know it!"

"You'll steal the show right out from under this Bryna Hissler," Leslie's father said. "Have you ever seen Leslie act, Peter?"

I shook my head. *And I don't especially want to,* I thought.

"She's incandescent!" he exclaimed. "Absolutely. You can't take your eyes off her. Even if she isn't speaking, she has such extraordinary presence, even in the tiniest role—"

"Oh, Daddy," Leslie protested weakly.

"No 'oh, Daddy.' This is the solemn and unvarnished truth." To me he said, "Do I look like a man who under any circumstances would say anything that was not the solemn and unvarnished truth?"

"No," I said.

"Wait till you see her," he said. "It'll be the experience of a lifetime."

"I don't like plays that much," I said.

Leslie's father looked taken aback. "Don't like plays? How can that be?"

"Most of them seem so phony. No one ever talks the way people do in plays. You can always tell they're acting."

"If by that you mean an element of artifice is a part of it, well, of course. But that's true in all the arts. What is real, after all? We all have our own definitions of reality."

"If I'm going to watch people act," I said, "I'd rather see a movie."

"You're such a philistine!" Leslie said. "Movies are idiotic."

God, Leslie is such an unbelievable pain! I can't believe we ever even liked each other, much less anything else. Maybe I was blinded by the summer light or something.

I took the train home and started inventing a scenario in my head about an imaginary girl who was waiting for me, pining away. She looked a little like a girl who liked me in seventh grade and then moved to Pittsburgh—Josie Gutman. Josie was slightly plump, and for some reason she thought everything I said was hilariously funny. She'd laugh and turn this marvelous shade of pink and squeal, "Oh, Peter, don't, really. Stop!"

Mom was at home, watching TV. "How was it?" she asked.

"Boring." I sat down in the chair to see what she was watching. It looked like an old war movie.

"I should call Preston. I've been meaning to. Is he all right?"

I shrugged.

"Maybe we should have him and Leslie out for dinner one night. How about it?"

"Leslie's a pain," I said.

Mom looked surprised. "I always thought the two of you got along so well."

"When we were kids maybe. Now she's really full of herself, with her acting and everything. She's turning into a real snob."

Mom was watching the TV. "I'm sorry to hear that," she said. "It could be Aline's influence, I suppose. But Leslie always seemed so different from her."

I went into my room and looked around for something interesting to read.

A minute later Mom looked in. "I heard from Muriel today," she said. "She said she'd be delighted to have me come and stay with her if I get accepted at Chicago. She has two bedrooms, one she only uses as a study, and she says there's no major man in her life at the moment. It might be fun, like old times, when we were rooming together."

"That sounds good," I said, not really interested.

"The only thing is, Peter, it might mean your living with Aline and Nelson for a semester, starting in January. You wouldn't mind that, would you?"

"What?" I stared at her in horror, disbelief.

"I'm sure you could transfer your credits, and if you get into Harvard on early admission, maybe they'll make allowances. You have such an outstanding record. You could do a work-study project or something."

I looked at her as though she was crazy. "Mom, listen, I'll live here by myself. I'm *not* moving into the city. That's final!"

"What do you mean you'll live here by yourself? I'm selling the house! That's the whole point! I need the money to live on while I get my degree. Peter, don't be absurd. Aline and Nelson have a giant apartment, or so I've heard. There's plenty of room for you."

"It's not a matter of room. Look, I'll stay at the Y."

Mom approached me, exasperated. "Stay at the Y! What are you *talking* about? Peter, you're supposedly the rational one. Why in the world should you stay at the Y?"

"I just don't want to stay with them."

"Will you give me one good reason?"

I couldn't. The idea of living under the same roof with Leslie—the constant erotic temptation, her acting snotty and aloof—was too hideous to think about. Yet I didn't feel capable of inventing anything else.

Mom's expression softened. "It's sweet of you to take my side," she said, "if that's what it is. But really, I wouldn't take it as a betrayal if you lived with them. You don't have to love them or even like them, either as a couple or individually. But I'd go crazy with worry if you were all alone somewhere. Just think of it as if you were boarding with them."

"Have you asked them about it?"

"No, but Nelson feels so guilty at this point that he'll do

anything I want." She bit her lip and sighed. "Peter, maybe this doesn't make sense to you, but I feel like right now I have this little bit of momentum, and I want to take advantage of it. I know it's really fragile, and if I wait even a few more months, I'll just sink back under the weight of inertia, and I'll never get out. I'm terrified of that!" Her voice was trembling.

"No, I understand," I said, backing down.

"Remember that woman they found on the train tracks a few months ago? It said in the paper that her husband had left her, she was petrified of the future, and she just, one morning she just . . ." Mom's voice broke.

I went over and put my arm around her. "Mom, you're not like that."

"I know, I *know* I'm not, but it's strange. This was way before I knew officially about Nelson and Aline, but even then, when I read that story, a cloud passed over my soul."

I tried to pull myself together. "Yeah, well, I guess I can hack living with them for a couple of months. Don't worry about it."

"Aline isn't . . . I mean, she's a deceitful person if she wants something you've got. I think she'd kill to get someone's job or husband, but there's no reason she shouldn't be a perfectly charming stepmother. You'll probably fall madly in love with her." She laughed bitterly.

I laughed too. "Not very likely."

Mom kissed me. "You're such a comfort to me, sweetie. But I really feel afraid that if we're together, I'll use you somehow, confide in you more than I should, drag you down. Your life's just beginning."

"Maybe yours is too," I said.

Her face brightened. "Do you think it is? Maybe. Oh, I hope it is!"

Casting Against Type

WE HAD A RUN-THROUGH OF THE PLAY, AND NOW, TWICE A week, we're doing individual scenes. I've watched Vladimir and Bryna a couple of times, and she *is* good. He's the problem. He's a total stick. Probably the best, just in terms of acting, is Mel as the father. It's funny, Mel is so short, and the father is supposed to be this rigid, authoritarian kind of person who rules and wrecks everyone's life. I had imagined him as tall and craggy, but when I did the long scene with Mel where he catches me with Captain Cook and interrogates me, forbidding me to see him, I got really scared. He grabbed hold of my hand and held it so tightly that I couldn't move. I have a line, "Is it nothing to you that I—that I shall hate you for this to the end of my life?" and he says, "Less than nothing." He spat it out so coldly and contemptuously that I felt chilled.

Brandemour called out, "Splendid! This is a struggle to the *death*, kids, nothing less. These people are not horsing around. This repressed society had hideous torments of feeling seething beneath its surface, and when it exploded to the surface, it *exploded!* I like your hate, Leslie. It's strong. Don't hold back."

I know that what's hard for me is playing someone who confronts people openly. I'd like to be that kind of person, but I just can't let it out. That's why I've always been friendly with people like Mira, who is so direct and honest about her feelings. Mira says she and her mother have had actual wrestling matches where they've rolled on the floor and pulled each other's hair. Once she pulled a whole tuft of hair out of her mother's scalp. And they scream at each other, "You stupid bitch!" But at the same time, once they make up, they're really close. They'll spend all weekend together, making brownies, going to old movies, talking about men and sex. I don't have either extreme with Mom. On the surface things are coolly hostile or coolly polite. Even with Daddy, whom I love a lot, we don't communicate that directly or even talk openly about what we feel.

After the scene with Mel I went to the bathroom before leaving for home. Petra Garland, who plays Arabella, and Bryna were in there, fixing their hair. Petra's gay and last year had the school in an uproar because she walked around hand in hand with her girl friend, Cindy, a senior who graduated last spring. She comes to school in hats with veils, spike heels, really tight jeans. They can't do much about it because she's one of the best students in our class.

"I think he's a child," Bryna was saying. She was rebraiding her hair.

"Well, he gets erections, I can tell you that much," Petra said, giggling.

"Who?" I said, going into one of the booths. I'd gotten my period that morning and was feeling kind of crampy and tired.

"Mel," Petra called out.

"How do you know?"

"We played that scene today where I sit on his lap, and there was just no mistaking it, baby."

Bryna let out a hoot. "God, you're awful! What'd you *do*?"

"I didn't do a damn thing," Petra said in her airy voice. "He's just a horny slob, like the rest of them. Can I help it if I'm ravishing and sexy?"

I came out of the bathroom and heard Bryna say, "You two are lucky. I feel like I'm going to die of embarrassment in most of those love scenes." She struck a pose. " 'Oh, Robert, I love you too well to let you waste your time pursuing the pale ghost of a woman.' "

" 'Waste your manhood,' " I corrected. Damn. Well, I *know* the part by heart.

Petra struck a pose like Browning. " 'Do you think I'm a boy to be swept off my feet by an impulse, or a sentimental dreamer blind to reality?' "

Bryna started giggling. "I think you're an idiot."

Petra looked at me. "Aren't I better than that fool of a Russian? *I* should have been Browning! I'm *made* for the part. I have more passion in my big toe than he has in his whole body!"

"P., lay off," Bryna said. "Vladimir's sweet."

Petra shook her head. "Wouldn't I have been better?" she asked me. "Be honest."

The idea was so bizarre I was taken aback. "I just can't imagine a woman in the part."

"Why not? Sarah Bernhardt played Hamlet. . . . I would have been a great Browning, but instead she casts me as this sickening, baby-talking little wimpette. I could kill her!"

"How do you think *I* feel?" I exploded. "I didn't want to be Henrietta!" I hadn't meant to say that in front of Bryna.

Bryna looked embarrassed. "She likes casting against

type. But I think I'm getting into Elizabeth. It's her relationship with her father that's the key, not Browning."

I thought of what Brandemour had said about Bryna and her father. All I remember is a story she once wrote for English, a dialogue between a father and a daughter where the father kept tormenting the daughter verbally, taunting her. I wonder at times if Brandemour isn't a sadist, though, making Petra, who's gay, play a sexpot, and me, who's so repressed, play a flamboyant mistress type, and Bryna, who's been on Outward Bound trips and goes skiing every other weekend, play an invalid poet who never leaves her room.

It was my day for having dinner with Daddy, so I took the subway downtown. Some afternoons if I forget, I still take that train. It's like there's a part of me that forgets that the divorce and remarriage ever happened.

During the week Daddy isn't much of a gourmet cook. He buys steaks and chops and heats up a frozen veg. He always lets me have the bone if it's a porterhouse. There's something comforting about gnawing on a bone, really stripping it down to the roots. But if I want dessert, I have it later on because he doesn't like sweets around the house.

"Do you feel like you're getting used to it?" I asked. "Living alone?"

"I've always lived alone," he said.

"No, I mean—"

"I miss you. That's the only meaning the divorce has for me. Aline moved out emotionally years ago."

I drank some water. "Didn't that bother you?"

"That's what marriage is for most people, two people sharing an apartment, staying together for the children, finding consolation, if they need it, however they can." He stared off into space with a melancholy expression.

"What do you mean—consolation?"

Daddy smiled. "Girl friends, boyfriends, depending on one's sexual predilections."

I stared at him. "But you didn't ever . . ."

"Oh, I had my occasional encounters—nothing profound, just friendships where we allowed it to go over the edge."

I was dumbfounded. Daddy has always struck me as totally not the type for affairs. Not that he's so unappealing I can't imagine anyone liking him, but he seems so self-sufficient. "Well, do you think you'll marry one of them?"

"They are all married . . . quite happily actually. At least no physical violence, just the usual atrophying of feeling. I doubt if any of them would have me, and I'm not sure it's really necessary. I've tasted the delights of matrimony for twenty-three years. Don't you think that's sufficient?"

My stomach was clenching into a ball. I didn't know if it was jealousy over Daddy's having loved, if that was the word, other women, or just dismay at the cynical way he speaks of human relationships. "Will it be like that for me?" I asked, trying to sound wry and light-hearted.

"Of course not," he said.

"Why will it be different? If human relations are as bleak as all that—why should I be an exception?"

"Because you're a beautiful, sensitive person, and you'll make it work." He was gazing at me with a dotting expression.

I didn't say anything.

Daddy stood up and came over and caressed my shoulder. "I'm infecting you with my melancholy. Hence loathed melancholy! Begone!"

"I'm afraid you're right," I said. "No one I know has parents who've stayed together or who are happy. It just seems so rare."

"It *is* rare," Daddy said. "Everything that is good in life is rare and therefore to be valued. You are rare, and therefore I cherish you."

Daddy went in to make coffee, turning on some chamber music on the radio while I got out my French homework. He brought in my cup of coffee and set it in front of me. "Good coffee is rare," he said, "Mozart is rare, clarity is rare—"

"Steak is rare," I said, falling into his joking mood, "when it isn't well done."

"Ah, but things can be rare and well done at the same time," Daddy said. "A seeming contradiction, but true."

I haven't been thinking about Peter that much since that horrible day three weeks ago when he came into the city. I really don't understand the way he's been acting since the summer. In one way he's like me: He keeps everything inside. But it seems like the part of him I don't like, that sneering, "I'm better than everyone" part, has just gotten total possession of him. That whole afternoon whatever I said, he'd look at me with such a contemptuous, aloof expression. I wish so, *so* much we'd never made love! It's not that I regret not being a virgin, but I wish I'd waited to do it with someone who was more experienced and more relaxed. Peter's so gnarled up inside. And I hate the way he looks now—not just his gaining weight, but his sloppiness. He looks like some bowery bum. His hair wasn't brushed, his coat looked like a cat had thrown up on it. Why doesn't he take some pride in the way he looks?

But still he seemed safely faraway in Westport until the next day, when, during dinner, Nelson said, "It looks like you're going to have a brother, Leslie."

I looked from him to Mom. My first thought was that Mom was pregnant and had had amniocentesis and therefore knew it was a boy. She's forty, but she still gets her period, so I guess technically it'd be possible. "Congratulations," I said awkwardly, raising my glass.

"Les, don't be silly," Mom said. "I'm a thousand years too old to have a baby, and I wouldn't even if someone put a gun to my head. Nelson just means Peter is coming here to live with us, right after Christmas."

"What?"

"It seems Hope wants a new start in life and is going to Chicago to get a degree in art history. She's put the house on the market."

"But how about school? He can't commute to Westport."

"He's gotten into Harvard," Nelson said, "on early admission, and they've said they feel his qualifications are sufficient. I may be able to find some work for him at Einstein College of Medicine in one of the labs. I have a friend who works there, and Peter claims he wants to go into science."

I really felt upset. "Why can't his mother stay till the school year is over?" I said. "It's just six more months."

"Hope is a very determined person once she gets an idea in her head," Nelson said dryly.

"She wants a new life," Mom said. "Why not? I'm delighted. And it's the best thing for Peter. He adores you, Les. You can introduce him to your friends, take him to dances, get him in shape."

"Mom, Peter and I don't have *anything* in common," I said. "I am not introducing him to *anyone*. This is a tough year for me, and that's more than I can handle."

"Peter'll be okay," Nelson intervened. "Don't worry about him, Ali."

"Darling, I'm not! I'm really looking forward to this. I've never had a son."

Nelson sighed. "He's a disaster area. I don't blame Leslie one bit. Why should she have to take him on as a charity case?"

"We'll put him on a diet," Mom said brightly. "I think Peter could look terrific if he lost ten or twenty pounds."

"He's been on every diet on earth," Nelson said impatiently. "He just gets up at night and eats everything he can lay his hands on."

"It's probably sexual," Mom said. "If he had a girl or a girl liked him . . ."

It's funny. Even though I agree with them, I hated the way they were talking about Peter. It made me extremely angry. "He's not *that* fat," I said.

"Of course he's not," Mom said. "He's just let himself go. Like Hope, really. It's all mental. Everything is. If I didn't work out every day, I'd be a disaster area too."

They beamed at each other in that way that makes me sick.

When I went back to my room, I couldn't work. All I could think of was how horribly unfair this was. The year had been bad enough with Mom and Daddy splitting up and me having to get used to Nelson. Now to have Peter thrown in! And meanwhile I have the play, I'll be going to college interviews. I went back out to the living room where Mom and Nelson were sitting, reading.

"Why can't he stay at a hotel?" I said. "Or with a friend? Why with us?"

Mom looked up impatiently. "Sweetie, why are you making such a terrible fuss about this? Peter's your stepbrother, he's only seventeen. He needs a *home*. He'll have his own room. You don't have to pay the least bit of attention to him if you don't want to."

"Of course I will!" I glared at her. "Three minutes ago you said I'd have to introduce him to all my friends, take him to dances—"

"Well, I was under the obviously mistaken impression that you and Peter liked each other. If that's not the case, then by all means go your own way, and he'll go his. New York's a big, lively place. I'm sure Peter will find plenty to do. I just don't understand your being so selfish."

Mom can get me madder than almost anyone on earth. "It's genetic," I snapped and went back to my room.

The next day I messed up in rehearsal. I kept forgetting my lines and acting so badly that I was almost afraid Brandemour would kick me out of the play. But instead, at the end she just said, "Leslie, dear, perhaps you're a little *too* involved. Vivacity doesn't mean hysteria. You're just a young woman with natural warmth and vitality. Don't force it so. It's there. Let it just burble naturally to the surface."

Right after rehearsal I had my second meeting with my college advisor. She recommended the University of Chicago, where she went to graduate school. She said it was an interesting, stimulating place, good for someone like me who likes city life. The other places I'm applying—Wesleyan and Haverford—are more rural and isolated. If only I hadn't done so rottenly on the math part of the SAT, I really think I'd have a much better chance. Mira, which is really incredible, got 800 on the English and 770 on the math. She says it doesn't mean she's a genius, just good at taking tests, but still.

I was sleeping at her house that night. Once we were in our nightgowns, I pulled one of her comforters up around me. "I *hate* this year," I said fiercely. "I'm not going to get into any decent college, I'm wrecking the play, and now Peter is coming to live with us!"

Mira looked at me in surprise. "I thought you liked him."

"When we were kids, we played together. That's all there is to it."

"I thought you once said you wished he'd ask you out." Mira never forgets anything. That's usually something I like about her.

"I don't!" I yelled. "He's fat and sloppy and condescending. Why would I have gone out with someone like *that*?"

Mira was silent. I always feel she can tell when I'm lying, whether I admit it or not. I looked at her sideways. "Actually I slept with him once."

"With *Peter*?" She laughed. "When?"

"This summer, but it's . . . I don't know. The first time was just because we were both high, and it seemed like it just happened. But after a while I thought we really liked each other."

"So what's happened since the summer?"

I pulled my knees up to my chest. "He's been acting weird since the divorce. Maybe it's that technically we're related now. But I don't think it *is* that. He's just gotten horribly fat, and the two times I've seen him, he's acted so detached, like he was this great brain and above everyone else."

Mira was frowning. "That's so strange, your having done it and never telling me. I'd tell *you* in a second."

"I would've if it had turned into anything. Now I feel like such a jerk."

"Just ignore him, then," Mira said.

"You can't. I can't explain it, but Peter, even when he isn't saying anything, just gets your attention. It's either—pity me or admire me. He doesn't *let* you ignore him!"

I didn't really think I'd explained it right. If I hadn't felt that Peter and I were falling in love over the summer and that he was understanding about the divorce, the way he's acting now would be more comprehensible and certainly a lot less painful. I want to excuse it by saying he's shy and hasn't had much experience with girls, that he wants me to pursue him as I did in the beginning. But shouldn't he start taking some active part after a while? He has to have known after the summer that I liked him. I feel like maybe he's already mentally looking ahead to college, and I'm a part of his past, a girl he fooled around with enough so he doesn't have to feel ashamed about being totally inexperienced when his friends talk about sex. I hate to think that all boys are so detached when it comes to getting sexual experience, but maybe it's true. It seems to me that all the girls I know get over involved, whether we show it or not.

Still, I'm a good actress, and I'm determined to handle the months he'll be living with us. Well, I'll be cool, polite, very busy, and just stay out of his way. It's up to him to make the next move. If he doesn't, then too bad. I won't!

Peter didn't actually move in till after Christmas. His mother hadn't sold their house yet, but she had a real estate agent handling it for her. He brought a few boxes of stuff but didn't even unpack most of it, just shoved it into the closet in the guest room, which will be his room.

I waited till Mom and Nelson went out that evening before I spoke to him. "I think the best thing is if we each sort of go our own way," I said.

"As opposed to what?" he said coolly.

"As opposed to putting on some big brother-and-sister, we-love-each-other routine. Let's just act the way we really feel."

Peter put his radio down on the desk. "That's how I always act."

I turned away. "Okay." I felt too fed up even to talk about it.

He followed me down the hall. "Last summer you were a real person, someone I could talk to. Now you just seem like a jappy little bitch."

I laughed. "Ethnic slurs? Tsk, tsk."

"Forget the jappy, then."

"Why should I? Any other insults, or can I go into my room to study?"

Peter really looked embarrassed. "Scratch the jappy. I just meant—"

"Peter, look, if you want to know, I think you're just an

uptight, snotty, suburban prep seen through a fun house mirror. I'll take jappy any day of the week."

"I didn't *mean* jappy." He got that woebegone look. "I just meant you seem so full of yourself, like you're deigning to even live in the same house with me, like it's some tremendous burden."

I wheeled around. "It is, okay? I don't get the whole thing. Why couldn't your mother have stayed around till spring?"

"She didn't want to. Do you think *I* like moving in the middle of the year? I *hate* New York, I *hate* living here, I hate everything about it."

His explosion took me aback. "Okay, well, look. You have this supposed job, so you just do that, and I'll go to school and—"

Peter pointed his finger at me. "That's exactly what I mean," he said.

"What?"

"'This supposed job.' I have a job, okay? A real job. Why call it a supposed job?"

"I thought Nelson just got it for you because he wanted you off the streets till June." I felt flustered because I wasn't really sure.

"Yeah, he did, but I happen to be working in the lab of someone who's extrememly likely to win the Nobel prize in a couple of years. *And* he's letting me work there because he thinks I'm terrific, amazing as that may seem to you. He isn't doing this out of charity."

"Great!" I said sarcastically. "Another feather in your cap. Early admission to Harvard, a Nobel prize winner, while we poor mortals struggle on our dreary path—"

"Jesus, you really make me sick," Peter said.

"It's mutual!" I screamed.

With that I gave up and decided a detached silence was the only way I'd survive the next few months.

PART III

Zigs and Zags

"YOU COULD'VE COME TO CHICAGO WITH ME," MOM SAID tearfully. "Maybe Muriel could have arranged a job for you there. But her place is so small. . . ."

"Mom, it's fine," I said. "I really like the job here. I'm getting a lot out of it."

Her plane was due to leave in a few minutes. She was all bundled up in boots and a duffle coat; the tip of her nose was red. "Will you come visit me?" she said. "I'll send you a ticket the minute I'm settled."

"Sure, I'll come." I hate leave-takings, and Mom's nervousness made it worse.

"Is it going all right with Nelson and Aline and Leslie?" She sniffed and patted her nose with a Kleenex.

"It's fine," I said. "It's just a place to sleep basically. I spend most of my time at the lab."

"Don't work too hard," Mom said. "You've done so

wonderfully in school. Relax. Have fun! Go to dances! Go out with girls!"

Oh, boy. Hope springs eternal. "I will," I said, choosing the easiest answer.

"I'm so proud of you, Peter," Mom said. "I just want you to be proud of me."

"Sure," I said. "I understand."

They began announcing her flight. I stood as Mom hurried through the gate, clutching her bag and looking back at me. Then I took a cab back to the apartment. After lunch I set off for the lab.

This job is saving my life. It's terrific. Harvard said they'd accept it as a substitute for second-semester senior-year classes. The guy I work for, Rex Rosenblum, struck me as extremely manic the first time I met him. He kept jiggling his foot, and his eyes darted all around the room while he made notes on a little pad. "I don't believe in these intern projects," he said. "What can you do in a semester? Not much. But I think it'll hook you. I was impressed by that Westinghouse project of yours—fine work."

"Do I have to sign on the dotted line?" I said. "I'm really not positive I want to go into research."

He grinned. "You'll go, you'll go. . . . But no, join the circus, whatever. I just sense after a few months here, your mind'll be made up."

"My father thinks medicine might be more practical."

"Your father!" He shrugged. "What does your father know? He's an actor. He may be one of my best friends, but never listen to a word he says. No one should listen to a word their father says."

"I rarely do," I admitted.

He rifled through some papers on his desk. "So, what kind of hours are you thinking of? We work a twenty-four-hour day around here. That's why we're all crazy and divorced. Our wives hate us, our girl friends scream at us, our kids don't know who we are. I hope you don't have any intention of having anything resembling a personal life. If you do, forget it. Either you live and breathe science from dawn to dusk, or you pitch it in."

I hesitated. "I want to give it a try." I looked at him. He had really dark gray bags under his eyes. He looked about a decade older than my father, though they're supposedly the same age. "Do you think you'll really win the Nobel prize? Dad said you might."

"Dad said! Is your father giving out Nobel prizes now? Are you asking do I deserve it, or will I get it?"

"Either."

"Yeah, I deserve it. Half-deserve it, anyway. You work, you work, and a few things turn out right. But not for the reasons you thought. People think of science as rational. Never! It's the unexpected zigs and zags that do it. You have to let yourself follow them." Then he outlined the project he wanted me to work on, a gene-cloning experiment.

There are three other people in the lab besides Rex and me: an Indian woman who doesn't say much, a pregnant woman with a big, booming laugh who's expecting twins in May, and a gay Englishman who's always going to the opera. I feel uncomfortable with the gay guy. Gay men frequently assume I'm gay. I really don't know why. Maybe I look too hopeless for any girl to like me. Also, I'm a good listener, and maybe they take that to mean I really like them.

But the main thing is that the lab gives me a place to be where everyone takes me for granted. I don't feel I'm on show or that I have to perform. Some days I don't talk to anyone, and no one cares. It's a kind of freedom I don't feel anywhere else. The other good part of being here is that I'll miss the second half of my senior year. I didn't feel like going to the prom or sitting around in classes I knew were useless. The high school agreed to accept my job for academic credit; this way they'll just mail me my diploma.

I've been living in New York six weeks now. Leslie and I have a truce, but it's a pretty hostile one basically. At meals we speak to each other as little as possible. One thing that got me furious was overhearing her mother say to her, "But at least try to be nice to him, dear! He has no friends, he's all alone." As though I were some Bolivian orphan from Save the Children! Leslie just snapped something like, "I'm as nice to him as he is to me, Mom."

One evening at dinner Leslie's mother, or Aline, as she says I should call her, said, "How about the dance on Friday?"

Leslie looked up sullenly. "How about it?"

"I was just thinking . . . perhaps Peter would like to—"

In unison Leslie and I said "No!"

Aline looked taken aback. "They're very nice dances," she said to me. "Everyone just pals around in a group. You don't have to be paired up with anyone special the way you did in our day."

"He doesn't know any of the kids," Leslie said, glancing at me sideways. "I don't think he'd have much fun."

"You can't tell," Aline said. "You never know when or where you'll meet someone. That's how I met Preston, at a party I didn't want to go to at all. My roommate had to drag me out of the house."

Leslie looked at me directly. "Do you want to go?"

"Not especially."

She turned triumphantly to her mother. "He doesn't want to. Listen, I have to call Mira. Am I excused?" Without waiting for an answer she flounced out of the room.

Aline smiled at me. "I'm sorry, Peter. Leslie can be a bit peremptory with the opposite sex. Don't take it personally."

I felt awkward. "Yeah, well . . ."

My father said, "Peter isn't much of an expert on those things himself."

"Oh"—Aline glanced at me warmly—"he'll be fine in college. It takes men longer than women, that's all."

I like Aline. I'm glad she wants me to call her by her name because she doesn't seem like a mother with a capital *M* the way mine does. It's not just that she looks younger and more perky for her age. Let's face it, she's kind of sexy. I don't know how much awareness comes from living here and seeing the relationship between her and Dad. At home he and my mother interacted as parents, but I never saw them interact as lovers or friends. Whereas sometimes I come home, and Dad and Aline are sitting in the living room talking, listening to music, holding hands, or she's lying with her head in his lap. When he walks into a room, her face lights up. He's less demonstrative than she is, but there's still quite a bit of touchy-feely stuff, enough to make me envious as hell. He's forty-seven—hasn't he had his share by now? How about me?

After dinner I read a letter from Mom which had come that morning. She seems to be doing all right, though she says she finds the classes really hard.

As I passed Leslie's room, I heard her rehearsing her part in the play. I have to admit I have this fantasy that she'll totally fuck up and forget all her lines on opening night.

The night of the dance I went out to a movie. That's something I like about New York. There are movies everywhere, hundreds of them, especially old movies. There was a great double bill at the Regency: *Notorious* and *Spellbound*. When I got out at midnight, it was raining, but I didn't care. I felt terrific. I wonder if women like Ingrid Bergman exist anymore. Maybe they never did. Maybe in real life she was just a stuck-up bitch, but, God, in some of those scenes where she brushes back that long, thick hair and speaks in that warm, throaty voice . . . Jesus.

Back at the apartment Leslie was in the living room, sitting on the couch with a guy. He was tall and good-looking in a brooding Heathcliff kind of way. They were making out or looked as though they'd been making out before I came in. "Oh, hi, Peter," Leslie said in a flustered way, jumping up. "This is Vladimir. He goes to Windsor too. He's in the play with me. Vlad, this is my stepbrother, Peter."

"Hi, Peter," Vladimir said.

There was an awkward pause.

"How come you were out so late?" Leslie said. She was wearing jeans and a fuzzy purple top.

"I saw some movies."

"Which ones?"

I told her. It was ironic that suddenly she seemed friendly and interested in me when during the six weeks I'd been here, she'd curled her lip if I'd even come near.

"Is *Notorious* the one where Claude Rains is a Nazi and has that witchy old mother?" Leslie asked.

"Yeah, I think she was in *The Lady Vanishes* too. Remember, where she wakes up on the train?"

"Oh, I love that one!" Leslie said. "That's one of my favorite movies. Have you ever seen it, Vlad?"

Vladimir looked a little out of it. "What?" he asked. Maybe he was just pissed because I'd interrupted them while they were making out.

Leslie looked at me. "Want some pot? We've been smoking some."

"Sure," I said. It was funny. Maybe it was just because it was our apartment, mine and Leslie's, but I felt as though the two of us were united against Vladimir, like Leslie's expression when she looked at him was sort of bored or mocking. I reached for the joint, and our hands touched.

Vladimir yawned. "I guess I really should go," he said,

looking uncertainly at me. Maybe he'd been hoping I might vanish into my room.

"It is sort of late," Leslie said, looking at her watch.

Vladimir looked at me again. "You never said you had a brother," he said to Leslie.

"He's a stepbrother," Leslie said, leaning back languidly. "Our parents just married each other this fall. My mother married his father."

Vladimir laughed. "Weird."

"Yeah, it *was* kind of weird," Leslie said, "but now we're used to it." She glanced at me. "Aren't we?"

I was already feeling mellow from the pot. "Sure," I said. "Leslie's a good little sister."

"Little! I'm two months older than you. Show a little respect, kid."

"Are you— Where do you go to school?" Vladimir said.

Before I could answer, Leslie said, "Oh, he's this genius. He's graduated already, and he's got a job in the lab of someone who's about to win the Nobel prize. Don't try to talk to him about anything because he's light-years beyond us mere mortals."

This mixture of making fun of me and boasting about me seemed so typical of Leslie. "It's just something to do till June," I said.

"Sounds great," Vladimir said. "I feel like I'm just marking time. I got into Harvard on early admission, and there's nothing left to study."

"Hey, so did he!" Leslie said. "Two geniuses! Wow. Two in one room. Maybe you can room together or something." She shook her head. "I think I'm getting slightly stoned."

Vladimir looked at her. "I told you it was strong stuff."

Leslie smiled vaguely. "Oh, I know my capacities." She glanced over at me again. "Do you feel it yet?"

"A little." I wished Vladimir would leave. He just kept standing there.

"So, look, are you going to stay or go?" Leslie said. "I mean, we don't care. But don't keep—"

"I said I was going," Vladimir said irritably.

Leslie jumped up to get him his coat. He called, "Nice to meet you, Peter."

"Same here," I murmured. I closed my eyes. I felt warm and good and sleepy.

Maybe I even dozed off a second because when I got back, Leslie was looking down at me. "Don't fall asleep!" she commanded.

"I'm not." I watched as she sat down at the other end of the couch from me. "Who was he?"

"I told you! He's in the play with me."

"He seemed like kind of a jerk." I took the joint from her and drew on it.

Leslie was silent for a moment, staring off into space. "He is," she said flatly. "He's a mean, stupid jerk. I hate him!"

"So why'd you invite him here?"

"I've always had kind of a crush on him—he's such a hunk. But then, right while we were making out, he said how he'd had some kind of bet with some of the other guys to see if I could act the way I do in the play in real life." She looked at me with an intense, defiant expression. "I'm not *like* that! I'm *not* a passionate, freewheeling person. Why do boys do that kind of thing?"

Oddly, I felt slightly as though *we* were in a play. Leslie seemed so upset and distraught, just as though she were playing a part. "Like what?" My voice came out slow and comforting, like a psychiatrist's, except I was the one lying down.

"Manipulative, seeing if they can play on your feelings . . . That horrible kind of detachment." She looked at me accusingly.

"*I'm* not like that."

"You are! You're *exactly* like that. Right now you're not even here. I feel like I'm alone in this room. You're just this body lying there. If I went jumping out the window, you'd just lie there."

I sat up nervously. "No, I wouldn't, Les."

"Daddy's like that too. He adores me, so he says, but he talks about women in such a cold, cynical, detached way. Why? What is it about? Is it having a penis? What makes men act like that?"

"I don't agree with you. I don't think they do."

But she went right on. "Maybe it's some hormonal thing. I mean, women, girls, just come right out and say what they feel. There's not all this stupid manipulating shit of trying to get things out of people. How do you think I felt? It was awful! I'm kissing him, thinking he likes me, and right in the middle practically he says it's all on a bet!"

"At least you weren't actually doing it," I said wryly. I felt some kind of perverse delight at this guy's taking advantage of Leslie practically at the same time that I was feeling sorry for her because she looked so upset.

She stared at me. "What do you mean, doing it?"

"I mean, say you'd been actually fucking, and he told you then. Wouldn't you have felt a lot worse?"

Leslie flushed. "I wouldn't have done that with him in a million years! God, what a stupid thing to say!"

There was a moment of silence.

"I'm sorry," I said.

"Sure," Leslie said bitterly. "Sure you are."

"I am," I repeated. My voice sounded a little wobbly, like a record playing at the wrong speed.

"Peter, please! You're sitting there gloating from head to *foot*. All you wish is that I was kneeling on the floor begging you to sleep with me. You aren't sorry one bit!"

I laughed nervously. "I don't think I'm gloating."

Suddenly Leslie kneeled near the couch and leaned

forward and kissed me. "You're gloating," she whispered. "Admit it. Gloat, gloat."

I guess pot affects everyone differently. The way I felt was that I was watching an interesting, slightly weird play in which both actors were saying and doing peculiar things. Part of me kept trying to connect and analyze everything the way I usually do, but it was hard. I'd get a third of the way there, and then it would all dissolve. I looked, entranced, at Leslie's face, which was so close to mine. "I just felt jealous of the guy. God, you look so beautiful when you're stoned!"

Leslie kissed me again gently, on the eyelids. "When *you're* stoned, you mean. That's what's affecting your perceptions of reality."

I felt so excited my body was trembling slightly. "My perception of reality is that we should—"

"But we're brother and sister," Leslie said softly, giggling, kissing me again.

"Who is who? Am I the brother?"

"It's all anatomical." She put her hand lightly over my erection. "I think you've got to be the brother."

"What about the parents?" I said. "They could come home."

"Right. Let us seek shelter in other quarters." Leslie took my hand. We went down the hall, kissing, to my room. "Your room is a mess," she pointed out.

"True," I said.

She walked into my room and without any further discussion pulled off her clothes and collapsed on the bed.

I slid in beside her, putting my arms around her. Her skin was soft and cool.

"We're not really brother and sister," she whispered. "We're what we always were, what we were before."

I saw the words *What We Were Before* in a lighted neon sign over our heads. Then we began making love, and all the words and connections vanished. I wasn't me, Leslie wasn't Leslie. Everything was slow, wonderful. My body was the way I always wanted it to be, strong, useful, graceful. It was easily the best moment of my life so far.

Afterward Leslie lay curled up against me. "It's wearing off a little," she said softly.

"It was wonderful," I said.

"Are you still gloating?"

"I never was."

"He humiliated me," she said, but quietly, without any of her earlier anger.

"Is that why you did it with me, to get even?"

"No." She hesitated. "It was . . . Suddenly you looked almost afraid of me, and I realized you aren't really that detached."

"No," I admitted.

She sighed. "But now it's all fading. I don't feel sure of anything anymore."

"Les, let's get married," I said to my own amazement. I felt electrified with certainty.

"We couldn't," Leslie said. "We're a million *years* too young. I'm not getting married till I'm thirty at least."

"Me neither," I said. "Probably I never will."

"I'm not sure we're that well suited to each other," Leslie said. "We're too much alike. And I have these moments of hating you, and they're pretty strong."

"Yeah. I have them about you too."

"But I've been trying," Leslie said. "I've been trying to be nice."

I stroked her arm. "This is nice. You didn't try this before."

"This is lust," Leslie said sternly. "Or something like that."

"I think I like lust," I said. "Maybe that's our strong suit."

Leslie half sat up. "What's strange is, I don't even know if I *like* sex. Sometimes I think I'll just be like Ms. Brandemour, sort of celibate and intellectual and intense, and I'll sublimate like mad."

"This is better," I said stroking her breasts. "Let's—"

Just then the front door opened. We heard Dad's and Aline's voices. "Oh, God," Leslie whispered. "They'll kill us!"

"Just get under the covers and don't move, okay? Can you do that?"

Without even answering, Leslie slid under the covers. I lay there, my arm over my eyes, steeling myself. A few minutes later Dad opened the door. "Peter?"

"Yeah?"

"Are you asleep?"

"Not quite."

He came into the room. "It smells like someone has been smoking pot in the living room. Was that you?"

"Yes," I said.

"You left one joint burning. That's dangerous, you know."

"I'm sorry, Dad. I forgot."

"I didn't know you were in the habit of using drugs. Is this a recent development?"

"No, I just . . . I had some saved from school, and it was kind of a rough day."

"I see." He hesitated. "I know life has been hard for you recently. Not that I see that as an excuse, but I'd far rather you indulged, as it were, at home, openly, than sneak off somewhere."

"That's what I figured," I said. I could feel Leslie's breath next to my knee. I was praying he'd get out and leave me alone.

"By the way, you don't know where Leslie is by any chance, do you? It's after one."

"Oh, that's right. I forgot. Ugh—she called and said she might sleep at her friend's house."

"Mira?"

"I forget. She wasn't sure, though. She just said not to wait up, that she was okay."

"Next time leave us a note, will you?"

"Sure, Dad."

He moved toward the door again. "Well, sleep well, Peter. See you in the morning."

As soon as he closed the door, Leslie slid up and peeked out from under the covers. "God, I was so scared that I'd sneeze! What should I do?"

"Wait a little while, till they're in bed."

"I need to go to the bathroom. Do you think that's okay?"

"Sure."

I wonder what my father's reaction would have been if he'd actually caught us at it. Not that I wish he had, but I guess in some way I would like to have him know I can get a girl. Maybe I'll have to lay in a stock of pot, if that's the way it affects Leslie. She was never like that before, and probably tomorrow she'll be the way she always is.

Once the house was dark and quiet, she got out of bed and bent down and kissed me again. "Let's just do whatever we feel like," she whispered.

"Sure," I said, not knowing what that would mean.

Trying Your Wings

THIS IS ONLY THE THIRD TIME I'VE PLAYED SQUASH WITH Nelson, and I beat him! When we were done, my heart was beating so fast I could hardly speak, and my body was drenched in sweat. He laughed and put his arm around me. "Leslie, you're incredible. My God, what coordination! I can't believe it."

"Did you let me win?"

"Are you kidding? I'm the most competitive bastard on earth. You're just so fast."

I grinned at him. "I feel terrific."

He squeezed my arm. "What a daughter! You *are* terrific. You know, we ought to enter the father-daughter competition here. Do you want to?"

"Sure, I guess so. This may be beginners' luck, though."

I went off to shower. We play at a club in midtown where they have a gym and a ladies' shower and sauna. I felt so high I couldn't believe it. Squash is really fastpaced, but for some reason I'm better at it than at tennis. The first time I thought it was too fast, but the next time I totally threw myself into it. It's too bad Peter doesn't like it. He tried it once and said he thinks it's insane, lunging around a little room, trying to murder your opponent. And, though I hate to admit it, I like the flirtatious undercurrent with Nelson while we're playing. I'm sure it's some depressingly familiar oedipal thing. I mean, sure, I love Daddy, but physically he's sort of hopeless, like Peter. Nelson is in excellent shape, and he's such a flirt. He touches me a lot, supposedly just in a friendly way, but I think he knows he turns women on and does it almost without thinking.

"I'm not that competitive," Mom said at dinner. "I like squash, but it seems so cutthroat, somehow."

Nelson grinned at me. "That's the fun of it. You should have seen Leslie. She's a demon."

Mom gave me a cool, appraising look. "She has a lot of intensity," she said, as though I weren't there.

Peter had been sitting silently, as usual, but I sensed he was irritated too. I think it's partly that it's hard to understand the sheer manic pleasure of intense athletic competition if you've never experienced it. I felt really glowing.

Ever since that night two weeks ago, Peter and I don't seem to know how to act with each other. The hostility and tension is gone, but what are we now? Lovers? Friends? I know I wanted to break through to him because I hated the way we both were behaving, but I also don't feel that ready to plunge into a real affair again. I'm afraid to be as vulnerable as I was over the summer and chance his turning away again. He says he was taking his cues from me, but I think it's more that if I feel really self-confident, I can reach out to Peter and not worry about what his response will be. But when I'm feeling, as I often do, uncertain, I can't do that. I want him to make a move toward me, and he just doesn't seem able to. It's his character, and even though I can accept it in the abstract, it's still hard to deal with in reality.

Despite that, it's such a comfort just having him around now. Peter senses and understands so much, even if he doesn't say a lot, I can just look at him and know I have an ally. I feel so much less alone than I did earlier this fall. It's funny how inviting Vladimir over led to my going to bed with Peter. It wasn't just the pot, though, that helped. It was that after having had such a crush on Vladimir from afar, I saw what a fool he really was, so full of himself, so uninterested in girls except on that dumb scoring level. Suddenly Peter, who isn't half as good-looking, seemed so wonderful! With Peter I feel there's a bottom level honesty. Even if he doesn't show his feelings that well or that often, everything is genuine. If only it weren't so buried, so hard to get to!

I glanced at Peter quickly, trying to gauge his reaction to my having played squash with his father. But he was just eating silently, eyes downcast.

"Leslie and I may enter the father-daughter competition," Nelson said.

"How can you?" Peter said. "You're not father and daughter."

Nelson looked irritated. "What do you mean? How are we not? Isn't Aline's and my marriage legal?"

"She's your stepdaughter," Peter said in a cold, angry voice.

"Stop being such an uptight logician," snapped back Nelson. "The fact is, I've never had a daughter before, and I intend to enjoy the one I have."

Mom looked over at Peter. "How about it, Peter? Maybe you and I should enter something together. I've never had a son either."

"It's just amazing," Nelson went on. "I have three sons,

and two of them watch their health, their weight, their appearance. But not you. You're young! Why not take pride in the way you present yourself to the world?"

"I take pride in other things," Peter said. "Like my mind."

"That's no excuse. Take Leslie as an example, Peter, now that we have this year together. She watches what she eats, she takes care of herself."

I wished Nelson would shut up. I could practically see Peter's hatred for him coming out of his hurt eyes and set mouth. Finally he just got up and left the table.

"You shouldn't go at him that way," Mom said. "He's terribly sensitive."

For once I agreed with Mom.

"He's just impossible," Nelson said. "Why didn't I make Hope take him with her to Chicago? He could get a job there. Why does he have to ruin our first year together?"

"He's not," Mom said. "We're having a wonderful year."

"We are not," Nelson said.

Mom turned white. "I—I don't see how you can say that. To me it's wonderful." She turned to me. "Aren't you happy, Leslie?"

"Sure," I stammered, almost scared at how devastated she looked.

"I've never been so happy," she said, her voice shaking. "What do you mean?"

"I'm just overtired," he said, looking away.

"You can't expect everything to be handed to you," Mom said. "You work for happiness, you work at it. It doesn't just happen."

There was a tense silence.

"I guess I'll have dessert later," I said.

I went into my room. Even though the door was closed, I could hear their voices going on, Mom's short staccato voice and Nelson's deeper one. It reminded me of the quarrels Mom and Daddy used to have when I was really young, when she would scream and slam doors. I remember then I had some obsession about whether to leave my door open or closed. I wanted to keep it closed so I wouldn't hear them, but I was also afraid a robber might climb in the window and kill me, and if the door was closed, no one would hear. Then the quarrels must have tapered off. I guess Mom and Daddy went their own way, and there were long silences and cool, brisk conversations, like between two lawyers on opposite sides of a case.

The only kind of marriage I've ever heard of that appeals to me is one in which both people have their own apartments and see each other on weekends, say, or maybe for a few days during the week. But that's probably hard if there are children. I feel sorry for Mom because I know she really loves Nelson and would be devastated if he left her. Not that he seems about to, but he's not consistently warm and loving with her the way he was in the beginning.

I took a long hot bath and felt better. As I was getting ready for bed, Mom came in and closed the door behind her. Her face still looked upset. "You mustn't start doing this again, Leslie," she said.

"Doing what?" I was puzzled.

"Playing up to Nelson at my expense, the way you did with Preston. Do you understand me?"

"No." But, although I really didn't understand, I felt instantly guilty.

"Nelson and I are in love, very much in love, and we agreed to take you and Peter because we wanted to include you in our happiness. If—"

I couldn't believe what she was saying. "Mom, what are you *talking* about? That I played squash with him? I won't anymore if you don't want me to. I won't enter that stupid father-daughter thing. It was *his* idea."

"Why don't you have boyfriends your own age?" she said. "It may *seem* easier to do this, but it isn't. In the long run, it will only bring you terrible unhappiness."

I really felt sick. Her face looked so tight and angry, like a mask almost. Every three weeks Mom has her hair dyed the same shade of golden red, and she's usually perfectly made up. But suddenly she looked older and tired, and I felt sorry for her. "I can live with Daddy," I said. "Do you want that?"

"Preston isn't able to . . . I don't think that would work. All I ask is some basic bottom-line consideration."

After she left, I lay in the darkness feeling worse than I had since that day when she told me she and Daddy were splitting up. I think what she said about me and Daddy is true. I did have a special closeness with him, and maybe it did exclude her and hurt her more than I realized. But it was Daddy who started it, from the time I was a little girl, and kept it going. I'm not saying I was an innocent victim but I was never consciously trying to hurt Mom. Still, maybe that's made her overly sensitive about the way I act with Nelson. And maybe I do flirt with him, more than I'm conscious of while it's happening.

I just couldn't fall asleep. At two o'clock I was still lying there, tossing and turning, trying to absolve myself of guilt. Finally I got up and went into Peter's room, closing the door behind me softly. He was sound asleep. I don't know exactly what I wanted. I just got in next to him and lay beside him, feeling so much better just from the warmth of his body and his bulkiness. I even dozed off a little until I heard him whisper, "Les?"

"Yeah?"

"How come you're here?"

"I—I just feel awful." My face was so close against his back that my voice came out all muffled.

He turned and put his arms around me. "Dinner was terrible."

"It wasn't just that." I tried telling him a little about the scene with Mom afterward, but when I was in the middle, I started crying.

"Hey, Les, don't cry," Peter said, keeping his voice low. "It's not your fault. She's just upset because she probably sees she made a big mistake marrying him. Your father's a lot better."

"She never loved Daddy," I said, trying to stop crying. "Ever! But maybe I was acting flirtatious with your father. Was I? Did you think I was?"

"He's just like that," Peter said. "He uses everybody all the time. God, I hate him!"

"I hate the way he treats you," I said.

Peter didn't respond.

"I love you," I said. I hadn't meant to. It just came out.

"I love *you*. Listen, in a few months we'll be free, out of here. We can do whatever we want with our lives."

"I know," I said, but I felt so uncertain, despite an excitement that we had "exchanged vows," that Peter, who's so reserved, had acknowledged what he felt for me. "I guess I'd better get back to my own room. Thanks for letting me stay."

He kissed me on the nose. "Any time. I thought maybe I was having a fantasy. I've thought about that happening a lot."

I blushed. "Well, if I ever have insomnia again . . ."

All the next day I thought about Mom. I used to think we didn't get along because I wasn't the way she was at my age, pretty, popular, good at sports. But now I think maybe she sees me as more of all of those things than I am. When I saw Daddy on Saturday, I tried to talk to him about it. I didn't want to mention my fear that I was flirting with Nelson just as I had flirted throughout my childhood with him. That seemed too potentially volatile a subject. Instead I brought up Mom seeming tense and unhappy.

"She's a queen who's losing her colonies," Daddy said.

"What do you mean?"

"Aline is losing her power—her looks, the ability to attract men, maybe some power at work too. You know, we all face that at middle age, sweetie, but I think it's hit her harder. You're blooming, she's fading."

I shuddered. "I'm *not* blooming! God, why do people *say* that? Don't they ever remember what it's really like? It's *hard* to be seventeen. I don't have packs of boys pursuing me. At school they all think I'm a weirdo. If it weren't for Peter—" That slipped out. I stopped.

"If it weren't for Peter what?" Daddy said. Like Mira, he picks up on everything.

"I just mean, it makes it a lot easier for me having him there too. Nelson yells at *him*, Mom yells at *me*. It seems to even it out."

"Would you like to stay here with me? I'd be delighted if you would. You know that."

If it weren't for Peter, I might have been tempted. I've thought of it a million times, but now I'd feel like I was deserting Peter, leaving him behind. "I can get through it," I said. "Peter and I are planning to fly to Chicago for my interview. His mother said we could stay with her."

"Give her my love," Daddy said. "I'm very fond of her."

My mind raced ahead to a new ending: Daddy would marry Peter's mother and live truly happily ever after, while Mom and Nelson . . . Well, I didn't let either side of the fantasy go very far, partly because it didn't really seem that likely, and partly because it seemed too cruel to be wishing Mom's new marriage wouldn't last.

* * *

Early in March Peter and I got ready to go to Chicago. I was glad to be getting away, escaping from the tension at home—glad to be having a little free time with Peter.

"Does Hope have room for both of you?" Mom asked. She had come into my room while I was packing.

"She has a sofa bed, and Peter's bringing his sleeping bag."

"I hope it isn't an imposition," Mom said. She was in her weekend jeans and a pale-blue cashmere sweater.

"She said she wanted us there. Really."

"It's nice of Peter to go with you," Mom said.

"He was going to visit Hope anyway," I explained. "I guess she must miss him a lot."

Now that things are so tense between Mom and me, everything I say seems to have two meanings. That came out sounding like I meant: She misses him, and you won't give a damn when I leave.

"Yes, Hope used to cling to Peter so much when he was a baby," Mom said. "I'm sure that's at the root of all his weight problems and feelings of inferiority."

I didn't think the way Nelson acts with him could have helped, but I didn't say that. "Of course, mothers are always blamed," Mom went on. "Either we overdo or we underdo. We can't win either way. At least I led my own life! At least I'm a person unto myself. That's what Nelson says he likes about me." She looked at me almost pleadingly, as though she wanted me to reassure her that she'd been a good mother. I wanted to, wanted even to try and explain about what had happened with me and Daddy, how I feel badly about the extent to which we excluded her. But I couldn't.

Peter peered into the room. "Ready yet?" We were supposed to leave that afternoon at two.

"Almost." Just then I realized that my cosmetic case was only half-packed, and my birth control pills were still in my top drawer. I reached in and scooped them up along with some scarves, which I stashed under my jeans.

"Are you bringing something elegant?" Mom said. "Hope may want to take you both out to dinner."

"I'm taking my black dress." I picked the black dress from a catalog. It's backless, which I guess is the only way to look sexy if you don't have too much on top like me. I always wear it with a choker of real pearls Daddy got me for my last birthday. In it I look as close to elegant as I'm capable of looking.

Nelson wasn't around when we left, and Mom was about to go out somewhere. Peter and I waited together while the doorman got us a cab. Suddenly I said, "Oh, damn, I forgot my nightgown."

Peter smiled. "Well, maybe you can borrow one of Mom's."

It didn't seem all that likely that we would do anything in Peter's mother's apartment and I wasn't sure I wanted to. Also, I was nervous about the interview, hoping to do well. On the Wesleyan one I had acted really dumb, just like one of those phony girls at school I hate. When the interviewer had asked me what writers I preferred, I said "Kafka," which isn't even true, and went babbling on about how I could identify with being a cockroach.

"You're really lucky," I said to Peter once we were in the cab. "It's all settled for you. You're into a good place."

"I'm glad too," he said. "Boy, I hope college is better than high school. I hope the kids are nicer."

"I think there are more different types," I said. I worry about that too. At least at Windsor I'm known. People think I'm smart, that I can act. I really dread the thing of starting all over, having to prove myself. I reached over and took his hand. "I wish I was smart enough to get into Harvard."

"Maybe if you have a good freshman year, you can transfer," Peter said.

We looked at each other, excited. I'd never thought of that. But a lot of kids do transfer after their first year. I thought that maybe if I worked really hard and got on the dean's list, they'd forget my SATs. But then I wondered if I'd really like that, going to school with Peter. College is supposedly a place to meet new guys, to try your wings. It could be claustrophobic having Peter around. "Well, let me get into one place first," I said, leaning back and closing my eyes.

Friendship Between the Sexes

"Muriel has a friend on the Admissions Board," Mom said. "Maybe she could—"

"Mom, Les is smart," I said. "She'll get in." She was having her interview while we waited for her at a coffee shop.

"She told me how worried she was about her SATs," Mom said. "I can really understand that. I was almost catatonic with fear when I took exams like that. And what do they show? Plenty of talented people do terribly on exams. Look at Uncle Morgan!"

Mom seemed pretty much the same to me, certainly not worse. The apartment she shares with her friend Muriel isn't much by Dad and Aline's standards, but it's okay. They each have a bedroom, and there's a living-dining room, where Leslie and I are sleeping. It's funny that if Leslie were my girl friend officially, Mom would no doubt make her sleep in another room, but this way she just rolled out the sleep couch, I took out my sleeping bag, and she said, "Good night, children," and closed the door.

Actually we didn't do anything that night because we were both pretty tired, but we lay in bed for a while kissing and holding each other. In a way I'd just like to go to bed with Leslie for the next year and forget about college and my job at the lab, everything. But she seems much more erratic about it. She can be warm and passionate and lovable, and then suddenly distracted and off with a million worries. I wish she were like me, that sex meant as much to her.

Mom said, "I think you *have* lost some weight, dear, haven't you?"

"A little." I have a plan that by June I'm going to be really thin. Maybe I'll fast one day a week. So far it hasn't worked that perfectly.

"I've lost some," Mom said. "If only out of worry. Peter, these classes are so hard! I'm so out of shape mentally. I haven't written anything but letters to friends in years, and suddenly I have to do a twenty-five page term paper on the French Impressionists. It's so terrifying, but exhilarating too, in a way."

"What'll you do once you get your degree?" I asked. "I heard teaching jobs aren't that easy to get."

"I know! Only I can settle anywhere now that you're all grown. And there's museum work. I don't know. I should, I guess, feel panicked at the unsettledness of it all, but instead I feel this tremendous excitement. Who knows, maybe ten years from now I'll feel grateful to Nelson for"—she made a wry face—"liberating me." She looked at me with concern. "Is it working out all right for you, Peter?"

"Sure, it's okay. There's a lot of tension, but I'm out most of the time."

Mom set down her coffee cup. "What kind of tension?"

I hesitated. "Basically between Leslie and her mother,

but just . . . I get the feeling they wish we weren't around."

"Well, parenthood was never Nelson's strong suit," Mom said. "I can't speak for Aline, but she always seemed so work-obsessed. Look, what can I say? I want them to be miserable, and I hate myself for being so petty."

"I don't think they're all *that* happy," I said. "But, like you said, it's a place to stay."

Mom looked at me with that intent "motherly" look again. "How about your social life? Do you go out at all?"

I laughed. "With who?"

"I thought Leslie might've introduced you to some of her friends."

"Mom, don't worry about me. I'm fine."

"I know you're fine," Mom said quickly. "I know in the *end* you'll be fine. Whoever marries you will be a very lucky woman. It's just that having someone who likes you, someone of the opposite sex, can be . . . well, it's an affirmation of a sort. It's important."

I turned red. "I know." A few quick scenes of me and Leslie in bed whisked through my head. Just then I saw her coming toward us.

Mom turned to look at her. "How'd it go?"

Leslie slid in next to me. Her face was flushed and excited. "I think it went really well. I think he liked me! He used to act himself, and he said he finally had to put that aside when it came time to earn a living, but he knew *The Barretts*. He'd seen it on stage. We had *such* a good conversation!"

"That's marvelous," Mom said. "Is Chicago your first choice?"

"Now I think it is," Leslie said. "They seem to have so many good programs."

"Muriel went here as an undergraduate," Mom said. "She can tell you all about it."

That night we went out to eat at a seafood restaurant. I wore a suit and tie. Leslie had on a sexy-looking black dress. She still seemed in a great mood because of the interview. Mom's friend Muriel is small and round with frizzy graying hair. "You're so lucky, the two of you," she said after we ordered. "I was one of five sisters, and I always wanted a brother to talk to about things. And then my poor daughter, Dorothy, is an only child, and she's never had a brother either."

"Dorothy is at Harvard," Mom said. She was sitting next to Muriel, opposite Leslie and me. "She's in her junior year."

"You must look her up," Muriel said to me. "I've told her all about you, Peter. She's going to get a doctorate in biology, so I think you two would have lots in common. Just a sec—I think I have a photo of her." She rummaged in her purse and came up with a snapshot, which she handed to me. Dorothy was, to put it mildly, a knockout. She had shoulder-length blond hair and a soft, almost sultry expression, a little like Ingrid Bergman's. "She just got contacts, and I think she looks so much prettier that way, don't you?"

"Yeah. She's gorgeous," I said sincerely.

Leslie snatched the photo away from me. "Well, she looks healthy," she said.

"She isn't." Muriel said. "She's had a *lot* of health problems, actually. Well, I'm glad you like her looks, Peter. Not that that's all that matters, but it does count to some extent."

Leslie was still glaring at me. "I thought you didn't like blondes."

"Who, me? No, I'm—" I started to say "omniverous" and then changed it to, "I have catholic tastes."

"Well, that's not what you *said*!" Leslie snapped.

"Dorothy was going with a lovely boy, but they just broke up," Muriel went on. "You see, she's very committed to her work, and she feels she must have a boyfriend who understands that. I thought someone else in science would understand."

All three of them were looking at me. "Sure, that sounds fine. I work pretty hard too."

"Dorothy must be terribly bright to get into Harvard," Mom said. "I heard they're even more discriminating about girls than about boys."

"Oh, she is!" Muriel exclaimed. "If she weren't so attractive, I think that might have given her problems."

"Surely we're beyond that," Mom said. "Men being scared away from women because of their intelligence."

"Now they're just scared, period," Leslie put in.

Mom smiled gently. "I hope not *all*!"

Leslie sipped her glass of white wine. "All the ones *I've* met," she said disdainfully.

Presumably that included me. I didn't exactly get her mood; she had seemed so happy in the afternoon.

"High school is so difficult," Muriel said. "But surely you'll meet someone in college who's more . . . Don't you think she will, Hope?"

"Of course," Mom said warmly. "You'll have scadzillions of boyfriends. I think Leslie looks very much like that actress we saw the other day—what was her name? Nastassia Kinski?"

Leslie said, "Some other people have said that."

"Don't you think so, Peter?" Mom asked. "Her eyes especially."

"Kind of." I was trying to be diplomatic.

Leslie snorted.

"But you know, romance aside," Muriel said, "I think friendship between the sexes is so important. Maybe *more* important. Don't you, Hope? And that's what the two of you have."

Leslie and I looked at each other. I raised my wineglass. "To friendship," I said wryly.

Leslie clinked her glass against mine. "To sex," she said defiantly. "Fuck friendship."

Mom and Muriel laughed nervously. "Well, a little of each would be fine as far as *I'm* concerned," Muriel said. "If you think it's hard for you, dear, try being our age."

"Someone tried fixing me up with a man my age who'd never been married," Mom said. "He spent the whole evening hiding behind a potted palm, he was so insulted. Evidently we're supposed to go into a convent after forty."

"I used to want to try and convert men like that," Muriel said, "show them the error of their ways. But now I just let them be."

I ordered a two-pound lobster, which was excellent. I decided to just concentrate on eating and forget Leslie and trying to figure out her moods. Mom and I shared a chocolate cheesecake for dessert, which was also delicious.

When we got back to their apartment, it was almost eleven, and Mom and Muriel said they were going to turn in. Leslie and I went into the living room and closed the door.

"Well, I guess your social life is settled for the next four years," she said. "Almost like computer dating. It sounds perfect."

"What?"

"Oh, forget it." She kicked off her shoes.

"You seemed in such a good mood this afternoon." I looked over at her. "What happened?"

"You looked like something out of *Porky's*!" she said. "It was really disgusting."

"Why can't I have cheesecake if I feel like it?" I said, slumping down on the couch defensively. "Chocolate's my favorite kind."

"I'm not talking about cheesecake, and you know it!"

Leslie said. "I'm talking about drooling all over that photo of that stupid Dorothy!"

"I was just being polite. I'll probably never even meet her."

"Oh? I thought the engagement was being announced tomorrow."

Suddenly I got the idea that Leslie was jealous. It seemed incredible, especially since I'd never met the girl and didn't even care about her. "Are you jealous?" I asked tentatively.

"Of what? Why should I be? I mean, let's face it, college is a fresh start for both of us. We'll both be dating new people."

"That doesn't mean we won't be seeing each other." I went over and sat down next to her. "I'll still love you." Leslie has said she never knows how I feel about her. That's hard for me to believe. I thought it was pathetically, almost ludicrously obvious, but evidently not. So I've been trying to put it into words more, which is hard.

Leslie didn't respond at first. Then she said, "Maybe we're just using each other."

"In what way?"

"Two oddballs, bereft of attention from the opposite sex, grapple a couple of times and call it love to clean up their act."

"That's pretty cynical."

"Look, we both got laid a few times. We have nothing to be ashamed of."

"Who's ashamed? It wasn't just a matter of getting laid for me, that's all."

Suddenly Leslie's expression changed. She looked at me searchingly. "Am I being awful?"

"Definitely."

"Did I hurt your feelings?"

"Of course!"

She rested her head on my shoulder. "I'm sorry. It's just

that I don't want to turn into some kind of perverse sex maniac in my senior year."

"Not a chance," I said, incredibly relieved by her change of mood.

"I mean, I think sex is important," Leslie said, "but it's also confusing. I haven't figured out *what* I think about it yet."

"Maybe you should stop thinking so much." I leaned over and kissed her. It was a long, tender kiss.

"Am I too smart?" Leslie said the second it ended. "Do I intimidate you?"

"Four hundred on your College Boards in math? Do I look *that* easily intimidated?"

Leslie laughed. "Kiss me again."

That kiss went on a lot longer. When we broke out of it, I looked up and saw Mom standing in the doorway. There was a long, terrifying silence.

"I just wanted to say I thought we might go to the museum tomorrow," Mom said. "It opens at ten, and we could have brunch there."

"Great," I said weakly.

"Sleep well," she said and closed the door.

Leslie fell on me. "Oh, no! Your mother liked me before this. Now she's going to think I'm some rotten slut, like Mom."

"Mom's not like that," I said, feeling uncertain myself. "And your mother's not a rotten slut."

"You're my stepbrother!" Leslie wailed. "What kind of person sleeps with their own stepbrother?"

I put my arm around her. "Les, that's just a technicality. That's our parents' fault, not ours."

"I don't know, Peter. I just think we should have some kind of control over our—"

"Baser natures?" I tried kissing her again.

"Peter, please be serious. What if your mother calls your father and tells him?"

"Are you kidding? They're barely speaking."

"Yeah, but she could try and make him feel it was his fault."

Leslie is great for getting me anxious, but I still tried to hold on to what seemed like common sense. "Les, relax, okay? Mom's a good guy. She may not even have seen us kissing. If she's not wearing her contacts, she can't see two inches."

"I didn't think of that. Do you think she's already taken them off?"

"Probably. Don't worry, okay?"

"Okay." We folded the couch out into a bed and went to brush our teeth. The door to Mom's room was closed.

As we got into bed, Leslie said, "I don't know if I'm in the mood."

"Let's just play it by ear," I said, reaching under the nightgown she'd borrowed from Mom.

"Don't you think I look at *all* like Nastassia Kinski?" Leslie said. "Not even a little?"

"You look a lot like her." I love Leslie's nipples; they're so round and soft.

"That's not what you said at dinner."

"I wasn't paying attention then." I began kissing her neck.

"Peter, I can't concentrate. You're getting me all excited. You said we'd play it by ear."

"We are. Here's my ear."

"That's your ear?"

We made love, and about halfway through I felt Leslie's mind dissolve and let go of worrying. It was funny. I felt like I was inside her mind and I could actually feel her let go, like someone dropping off a rope and falling into space.

The next morning Mom didn't make any references to

Leslie and me. I guess she really didn't see anything, just figured we were having an intense conversation. I think people see what they want to see basically.

At brunch Muriel and Mom asked Leslie about the play and how she liked being in it, and she went over the whole thing about having wanted to be Elizabeth Barrett Browning. "But there's a girl who's gay who wanted to be Browning," she said, "so I guess no one got the perfect part."

"Well, Hope and I may fly in to see it," Muriel said. "I'm planning on visiting Dorothy in the spring in any case."

"I couldn't act if you put a gun to my head," Mom said. "I was always so amazed at Nelson and Morgan, Morgan especially. One day he played Hamlet and Ernest in the Oscar Wilde play consecutively. He has such incredible range!"

"How is he?" Leslie asked.

Mom looked away. "Not at all well. I don't know how much more time he has."

I thought of the summer and Leslie and her father playing Scrabble with Uncle Morgan. Probably it was his last summer there.

At the museum we looked at a Picasso retrospective, but I didn't pay much attention to the paintings. I kept thinking of last night and the way Leslie can switch back and forth so quickly from one mood to another. It scares me sometimes because it seems to happen without any warning. Each time we resolve it, I think it's resolved for good, and then a few days later something makes her flare up again. But as we walked through the show, she talked to my mother, and her face had a calm, contemplative expression.

Feminist Studies

I FELT BETTER ABOUT COLLEGE AFTER MY INTERVIEW AT Chicago. I think it went well. I think I'll get in. Though the idea of a beautiful New England campus is appealing, I think I would miss a city atmosphere. Chicago doesn't seem as exciting as New York, but it's enough like it so I'll feel at home.

This semester I'm taking a course called Feminist Studies. I like it. Our teacher, Annie Mason, is young and lively, just out of college, with freckles and rimless glasses. She said we should call her Annie. But today I felt uncomfotable during the whole class, especially at the end. It started because Annie asked us to define a feminist, and everyone thought it was something different. Petra got up and said Gloria Steinem wasn't a "true feminist" because she wore makeup and streaked her hair.

"I think that's so superficial," Mira said. "Makeup is for a million reasons other than attracting men."

"Such as?" Petra wanted to know.

"It's theatrical," Mira said. "Like, some mornings I wake up and want to look like one of the Three Musketeers or Garbo or whoever. Makeup's a fun way of changing your identity. I don't think men even notice it half the time."

I was glad Mira said that because I love makeup, eye makeup especially. I think looking natural is fine if you're really confident about your appearance, but I'm not, and with eye makeup I look so much better. Annie told us about one of her sisters who was a nun and who said that even in the convent women were concerned about how they looked, even though they were brides of Christ. "For many women it's a reflection of how they feel about themselves," Annie said.

"If they feel they're nothing without makeup, that's because they've been conditioned by society to think they're shit. That's what our society thinks of women. Women love each other for their inner selves." Petra looked at all of us challengingly.

What's ironical is that most boys, I'm sure, would think of all of us as feminists, yet Petra doesn't think we go far enough to be real feminists. But it wasn't the makeup controversy that bothered me. It was when someone else offered a definition of a feminist as someone who wasn't sexually dependent on men.

"What does dependent mean?" I asked nervously. "Does it mean you have to be gay?"

Petra said it did, but Alida Hirsch said you could be sexually involved with a man, but not dependent on him.

"Could you explain that, Alida?" Annie asked her.

Alida is tall with curly black hair and slightly protruding teeth. "Well, like I have a boyfriend, and we have good sex and all, but my life wouldn't go to pieces if we broke up. What I mean is, we like each other, and sex is important to both of us. But I'm not grovelingly dependent in some demeaning way."

Annie encourages us to talk personally about ourselves if we feel it's relevant, but I find it's hard. "How can you tell the difference, though?" I asked, trying to act as though it were just an abstract issue. "How can you tell if you're dependent?"

Byrna raised her hand. "If you feel sick if you don't hear from him, if you see him with another girl and want to die, if you think about going to bed with him when you should be doing your math homework . . ."

Everyone laughed.

"That sounds like a very common problem, judging from the response," Annie said. "Is it?"

It was like most of the FS classes: The discussion was interesting, but nothing was really resolved. I suppose everyone has their own definition of feminism, and if it's important to you to think you are one, you twist it around to suit yourself. But I hate the way I feel so dependent on Peter! I *hate* the way I got so jealous about that Dorothy over the weekend. Peter claims he feels the way I do, that I have power over him too and that when I'm angry, he feels really upset, whether he shows it or not. But that's the thing. He never *does* show it! He keeps everything in so much, and that seems to give him some kind of advantage over me.

I wonder what it is about sex. Is it hormonal or what? You're doing this thing, this act, and yet somehow it becomes so gigantically important. Sometimes in class I find myself thinking about Peter, daydreaming about moments in bed with him. At night I even dream about him! I feel close to Mira, we've probably talked about more things than I've ever discussed with Peter, but there's none of that sense that if she stopped being my friend, I'd want to die. I hate that!

On the way home Mira said it wasn't worth worrying about, that my feelings of dependency were natural, and that Petra was too much of an ideologue. "Listen, when am

I going to meet Peter?" she said. Ever since she found out we were sleeping together, she's wanted to meet him.

"How about this weekend?"

We agreed she'd come over Saturday for dinner, and the three of us could sit around and talk or go to a movie, whatever we felt like.

When Mira showed up Saturday, I tried to remember what she'd said about makeup being for fun, not just to attract guys. I tend to forget Mira's looks, partly because I'm used to them and partly because in school she doesn't get herself together too much. But this night she had on tons of gray-green eyeshadow, a big slouchy hat, very tight jeans, a huge bright-turquoise velour top which just grazed her hips, and three-inch high-heeled boots. When I opened the door, she winked. "Dressed to kill," she said, laughing.

I had the feeling she had had a few drinks before she came. Mira says her mother is "sort of" an alcoholic, and sometimes Mira drinks to keep her company. She claims they can both handle a lot without seeming drunk, and that's true. I've even seen Mira come to school high and wouldn't have known it except for the fact that she told me. The only part I don't like is that it brings out her "theatrical" side more than usual. I had thought of the evening as the three of us sitting around, so I was just in jeans and a sweater, nothing fancy. I took Mira's coat, and she swept past me into the kitchen.

Peter was in there making clam sauce for the spaghetti.

"Hi there, Peter!" Mira said. "I'm the fantastic Mira you've heard so much about."

"Do you like clam sauce?" Peter asked, chopping imperturbably.

"Sure, I'll eat anything," Mira said, dipping her finger into the bowl.

Peter smiled at her. "Good! This is going to be a great meal if I may make a modest prediction."

At dinner we really pigged out—spaghetti, garlic bread,

red wine, salad with blue-cheese dressing. "So you're some kind of scientist?" Mira said. She'd kept her hat on during dinner, dipped seductively over one eye.

Peter explained about the experiment he was working on, something about gene cloning. "I'm still trying to extract the DNA," he said. "It's a pretty complicated process."

"But does that mean you'll end up cloning *people*?" Mira said. "Isn't that dangerous or immoral or something?"

"No," Peter said patiently. "This is just with fruit flies. It may have implications for human problems, but that's a long way off."

"Yeah, but here's the thing," Mira said. "Shouldn't you start thinking about the long term implications right *now*? Because look at those guys who built the atom bomb. They probably said the same thing. Don't worry now. And before they knew it, millions of people were killed!"

Peter poured himself another glass of wine. "All knowledge can be misused," he said. "There wouldn't be any science at all if everyone were that frightened of where it would lead."

"I guess," Mira said. "My father was a scientist, which is maybe why I have this prejudice. He was such an uptight, mean, detached son of a bitch. But you seem kind of nice."

Peter smiled ironically. "Thanks."

"I mean, compared to some of the creatures this one has been involved with, you deserve the Nobel prize," Mira said.

"Like who?" Peter said, smiling.

"Mira, come on," I said. I wished she hadn't put away a third of a bottle of wine on top of whatever she'd had before she came.

"That weirdo professor we had two years ago who thought Les reminded him of a pre-Raphaelite painting. That was *before* she cut her hair . . . And there was the guy at the dance. Remember, Les? The one with the moustache who thought *Swept away* was the greatest movie ever. Or—wait—remember the one who—"

"When are you going to take your hat off?" I said, feeling really pissed. If I started listing the guys Mira has been involved with, it would go on all night.

"What have you got against my hat?" Mira said. "How about you, Peter? Don't you like my hat?"

"It's a great hat," Peter said solemnly, staring at her.

"See!" Mira said triumphantly, waving her hat in the air. "Great hat, great girl!"

"I thought you dressed for yourself, not for men," I said loftily.

Mira laughed. "Is this Feminist Studies or what is euphemistically called real life?" She walked over to the hall mirror. "Mira, Mira, on the wall, who's the fairest of them all?"

I walked up behind her. "Cool it, okay?" I muttered.

Mira took her hat off and handed it to me. She shook her head, and her waist-length blond hair flowed out. "Happy?" To Peter she said, "My main aim in life is to make this one happy. She's so hard to please."

"Tell me about it," Peter said.

"She can be *so* critical!" Mira said, going into the kitchen after him. "There are some days when, no matter *what* I do, she gives me this stare." Mira imitated me, giving the stare.

"You're making me feel terrific," Peter said. "I thought it was just me. I thought maybe—"

"No," Mira interrupted. "The kid's a bitch sometimes, but it's out of love. She loves us just like we love her. Right, Les?"

"No!" I yelled. "Wrong! I think you're both acting like jerks, and I wish you'd both go home."

Peter looked at me plaintively. "This *is* my home."

Mira hugged him. "Oh, what a sweetie. Peter, is Les

your first serious affair? Tell us about your love life in—Where was it? Westport? Do they do it in Westport?"

"Mira, will you shut *up*," I said desperately. Peter is so private that I was sure he would just leave the room.

"Leslie *is* the first," Peter said, measuring water for coffee. "Girls and I never . . . we didn't connect."

"Golly," Mira said thoughtfully. "First love. Yeah, I know. It's a killer. Remember Jacques?" she asked me.

"No," I said sarcastically. "Who was he?"

But Mira just turned back to Peter. "When I was fifteen, I was on the Experiment, and I met this adorable French guy my age. I mean, he was the brother, quote unquote, in the family I stayed with. And it was really convenient because the parents slept on the first floor, and we were both on the second. So one night I kind of jumped him, in a quiet, demure way. And it was, well, it was a *great* summer!"

"Fifteen," Peter said, whistling. "That's pretty impressive. I was still putting wooden airplanes together at fifteen."

Mira smiled dreamily, twirling her hair around her finger. "I guess I'm a hedonist," she said. "See, if I do what I want, at least I know I'll please myself. Which is more than my mother, who's spent her whole fucking *life* just trying to please other people."

"You seem like a very open person," Peter said, looking at her sweetly.

"I am," Mira said. "I just say and do what I really feel. This one holds it all in, except on stage."

"You're such a phony, Mira," I said, furious. Why did she keep calling me "this one"?

Mira looked innocently at Peter. "Am I acting objectionably? Tell me. 'Cause if you think I am, I'll leave right this second."

"You're superb," Peter said. "Hey, Les, why don't you finish your wine? You don't want it to go to waste." He was speaking in a slow, slightly slurry way.

"We're having coffee," I said. "I don't *want* wine. I don't want to get drunk like both of you."

"She thinks we're drunk," Mira said. "*I'm* not drunk. Are you, Peter?"

"Maybe just a little," Peter said, "but I still have command over my . . . intentions." He went over to me. "Les, speak to me. Are you okay?"

I turned away. I felt so hurt at the way both of them were acting, I wanted to cry.

Mira said, "She thinks I'm flirting with you. I'm not! Am I flirting with you, Peter?"

"No," Peter said. "And even if you were, it wouldn't matter. Because your intentions are . . . pure."

"See!" Mira said. "He loves you, Les, you love *him*. What more does the kid want?"

"I want both of you to drop dead!" I yelled and ran into my room and slammed the door.

I had that horrible sensation of being slightly drunk, so that everything I felt seemed magnified and distorted, but not so much that I was over the edge and nothing seemed to matter. I wished *so* much I hadn't told Mira about Peter. For all I know, they were in there making out. Great! Let them. I decided to just go to sleep and wait till it was over.

There was a knock on the door. "Les?" It was Peter.

I didn't answer.

He opened the door. "We thought you might want some coffee," he said in his gentle, grave way. "There's cake too. And fresh strawberries."

I turned away. I was lying on my bed in the dark. "I'm not hungry."

He put his arms around me. "We don't want to just make pigs of ourselves all alone."

I sat up and looked at him balefully. "Then why did you act like that? It was so stupid!"

"I know," Peter said contritely. "But we didn't do it to . . . Come on back in. Please."

I went back to the dining room. Mira was at the table, dipping strawberries in sour cream. She was wearing her hat again. "I was a jerk," she said. "I'm sorry."

"I wanted you both to like each other," I said shakily, sitting down.

"We do," Peter said.

"But not, like, in some deep, passionate, lustful way," Mira said. "Peter thinks I'm gorgeous because I am, and if he didn't, he'd be a schmuk, and I think he's a sweetie because he is, but that's different from—"

"Okay," I said. "I get it."

I've known Mira long enough to know that she always does this act with boys. She says that it's because her father ducked out on her and her mother when she was so young that she just can't think of guys as people. All she can do is try and seduce them. She claims even when she knows she's acting like an ass and doesn't even *like* the guy, she just can't stop. Also, Peter is so totally not Mira's type that I knew she wasn't going after him seriously. She tends to like intense, flamboyant, emoting men—the kind who strike me as dishonest and unreliable.

I hated seeing Peter flirt with anyone—I never had before—but I have to admit he was really just catching the ball and tossing it back to her. So I made myself calm down and resolved to stay that way for the rest of the evening.

We were still sitting there eating strawberries when Mom and Nelson came home. He smiled at Mira and me. "Hi, girls, hi, Peter. Have a nice evening?"

"The kitchen's a mess, Mom," I said hastily, jumping up. "We're about to clean up."

Mom shot a look into the kitchen. "I want everything the way it was before you started. Pots, pans, everything. God, how much garlic did you use? The whole *house* reeks!"

"It was my garlic bread," Peter said. "It's a special recipe."

They disappeared into their end of the house. Mira looked after them. "What's bugging your mother?"

I shrugged.

"What is he—making it with other women or something?"

"No! Mira, hush. They just got married a couple of months ago."

"He's the kind who never stops," Mira said. Then she looked at Peter. "Oh, I'm sorry, Peter. He's your father, right?"

"Technically," Peter said.

"What do you mean? Did your mother have a lover? Aren't you legitimate?"

"I just meant I don't feel any special rapport with him based on family feelings," Peter said. "He's pretty much of a bastard in terms of human emotions."

"Huh." Mira looked woozy. She swept back her hair. "Why'd your Mom marry him?" she asked me. "Is he a good fuck?"

I threw a strawberry at her. "How am *I* supposed to know? Yeah, he probably is."

Peter looked stricken.

Mira threw a strawberry back at me. "Yeah, that kind is. What a shame. Still, at least she has that. Mom says my father did it in one second, and—which is weird because he was so tall—he had this *tiny* penis. *Really* tiny, she said. And, like, they say size doesn't matter, but she told me she didn't even *feel* it. Isn't that weird?"

Peter had turned bright red. He looked like he would have paid a million dollars to be transported to another planet.

Mira looked at him in surprise. "Listen, I'm not saying . . . I don't have that much basis for comparison. It's not size *per se* . . . but she couldn't even feel it!"

I leaned forward. "Hey, Mira, could you . . . I mean, they're in the next room, and these walls aren't a foot thick."

"Look, I hope your Mom's happy," Mira said. "I really do. And if your stepfather's a good fuck, more power to him, right? I mean, who am I to cast stones at a guy if he's got a little one or a huge one? Peter, don't take any of this personally. I'm sure whatever you've got is great."

"Uh . . . I feel a little funny," Peter said and lurched off to his room.

After he'd left, I said, "Okay, out! You've embarrassed him to death. What was the point?"

Mira threw her arms around me. "I think he's sweet. I wish I had someone. Do you think I ever will?"

Even though I knew it was being drunk that made her suddenly so vulnerable and weepy, and even though part of me was still furious at her, I hugged her back. "Sure, you'll find someone."

I even went downstairs and put her in a cab.

The next day Peter was silent and withdrawn and spent most of the afternoon hunched over his typewriter, trying to write up his experiments. Around four I went into his room, closed the door, and said, "Hey, it was embarrassing for me too. I hope you realize that."

Peter whirled around on his typing chair. "Is that how you talk about guys? Penis size? You sounded so technical and cold-blooded."

"No! Mira was just showing off. And since you spent the first half of the evening drooling all over her, she probably felt anything went."

Peter ignored that. "I never even thought to worry about my anatomy."

"I thought boys did," I said. "In locker rooms and stuff, that they compared and all that." I went over and kissed his neck.

"Not me," he said glumly. "I never thought about it."

"Anyway, she wanted to meet you, and you said you wanted to meet her, and it's over, and we both survived."

He was silent, brooding. "I guess it's just that I want to think that whatever happens between us is a private thing, not that the two of you go yapping away about—"

"We *don't,*" I said. "I didn't even tell Mira we were doing it till a few months ago. But I had to tell someone."

"Why?"

I looked at him, puzzled. "Just because . . . it's important. And Mira and I have always talked about private things. She told me about Jacques when it happened."

"I haven't told anyone," Peter said.

"Okay! So maybe boys are different. Maybe you don't *need* to tell. That doesn't make you better or morally superior."

Peter still had that grim, tight-lipped expression. "I feel like I've shared certain things with you that are really important to me. And now they're dispersed to all and sundry."

"Peter, I told *Mira,* that's all. No one else. No all and sundry. And we never discussed details. I just wanted to tell someone how I *felt.*"

He sighed. "Okay."

I went over and kissed his hand with a mock penitent expression. "Am I forgiven?"

"Sure. And I'm sorry if I acted like a dope last night."

I let him go back to his typing, feeling a lot better.

Ken

KEN IS BACK. HE'S BEEN AWAY THE WHOLE YEAR, TRAVELing around the world. He's not big on letter writing, so all I got were a few cards. Then, at the end of March he called from the airport saying he was on his way to Chicago and wondered if he could spend the weekend with us in New York. I realized he'd never seen Aline and Dad together as a couple. Everything has happened while he was away. But even if he'd been here, I doubt that he'd have been thrown by it the way I was. He always seems self-contained in a way I really admire. Whatever happens, he seems to accept it without taking sides.

When he walked into the apartment, I almost didn't recognize him. He'd grown a beard, and it totally changed the shape of his face. He looked thin and tan in jeans and a jacket; all his stuff was in a duffel bag, which he had slung over his shoulder. Aline came forward and said hello. "It's wonderful you can spend some time with us, Ken."

"Hi," Leslie said. "I'm Leslie. I don't know if you remember me. I—"

Ken smiled. "Sure, I remember you. But you used to be three feet tall. Hi, Dad. How goes it?"

"Pretty well," Dad said. I don't think he and Ken are especially close, but they never argue either. I think he respects Ken, even though their values are totally different.

Over dinner Ken told us about his trip and showed us the photos he'd taken. He's an excellent photographer, almost professional.

"Are you going to finish up your B.A. at Chicago now?" Aline asked.

"Definitely . . . I just needed this time off. It really cleared my head," Ken said. "Now I'm raring to go again."

"You're still going to major in philosophy?" Dad said.

Ken nodded. "I might even go on for a doctorate if I can rustle up some fellowship."

"But where will you get a job?" Dad said. "Teaching's dried up completely."

"I'll find something," Ken said. "Hey, that's great about Mom going back to school. I feel really proud of her. And I'm glad she picked a place where I can see her."

There was an awkward pause. "Yes, I gather she's managing," Dad said stiffly.

The next day I took Ken up to the lab with me. He had been a physics major before he switched to philosophy, so he could understand the experiments I'm doing and seemed interested. "I guess it's hard to miss senior year, though," he said.

"Not really. I was glad to get out," I admitted. "This is a lot better."

He picked up a pencil from the table. "I thought of coming back for the wedding, but I was in India and . . .

I guess I had pretty mixed feelings about it. Mom's really doing okay, though?"

"Sure." I told him about Leslie and me visiting her. "She says maybe it'll end up being the best thing that ever happened to her."

Ken was staring out the window. "I don't blame Dad. Things have been rotten between them for so long. But—"

"I never thought they were that rotten," I said.

"Don't you remember all the fights they used to have?" he asked. "All those times he stormed out of the house?"

"Yeah, I guess so. I wasn't really paying attention. I've always just tried to steer clear of Dad. He acts like I'm a total disaster, and nothing I do seems to change that."

Ken put his hand on my shoulder. "You seem a lot more together than when I left."

That could have been an opening for saying something about Leslie. I remembered how she's said after Mira came over, "I had to tell someone." I feel really conflicted about it. A part of me wants to tell everyone on earth, especially Dad and everyone who ever thought I was a fat little jerk who'd never get a girl. But basically I like the idea of no one knowing, of its being a private thing I can carry around and feel good about.

"I met a woman in India," Ken said. "We got pretty serious actually. But I haven't said anything to Mom or Dad."

"Is she still there?" Ken never had girl friends in high school, but he had friends who were girls who came over a lot.

"No, she lives in Chicago, which is convenient. The thing is, first she's thirty, and second she has three kids. Her husband split a couple of years ago."

Ken's just twenty-one. It's hard to imagine him with a woman ten years older. "What's her name?"

"Samantha. We're going to live together once I get back.

She has a house with an extra room, and I like her kids. Three boys, just like us."

I looked at him, trying to imagine it. "So, uh, are you thinking of . . . or is she just, like, a friend?"

Ken laughed. "It's the real thing. It finally happened. I was beginning to wonder."

"How do you know it is?" I asked, thinking of Leslie again.

"You just do. I don't mean in a flash, like a bolt of lightning. But there's a certain fit. You just don't have to explain or fill in. It comes together. Sam said she felt the same way, even though she'd sworn to her best friend she'd never fall in love again, and she doesn't like guys with beards. When she first saw me, she thought I was some hippie left over from the sixties, seeking inner peace. But it turned out she was over there just the way I was, wanting to find out something about Eastern culture. I feel like I've found a sister and a lover in one person. It's fantastic!"

I felt my heart plummet. *A sister and a lover in one person.* Yeah, I know. Why couldn't I tell him about Leslie and me? "It sounds fantastic," I said.

On the way home he asked if I was going to go into research.

"I don't know yet," I admitted. "Those guys work incredibly long hours, and most of them get booted out in a couple of years if they can't get grants."

"Nothing's that secure anymore," Ken said.

A funny thing happened on the subway going home. It wasn't too crowded because it was only three o'clock. I noticed a girl staring at us. Finally she came over and said to Ken, "I know this is kind of rude, but my girl friend and I were wondering if you're the man who does the weather report on Channel Four?"

Ken laughed and shook his head. "I've been traveling

around the world for the last year. It would have to be my identical twin, and as far as I know, I don't have one."

The girl kept staring at him. "It's really amazing how much you look like him."

Ken seemed embarrassed. "That's life, I guess."

"Do you work in the city?"

"No, I'm just passing through. . . . This is my brother, Peter."

The girl shook my hand. "Well, we just wanted to say . . . I mean, I realize this sounds strange, but if you felt like joining us for dinner, me and my friend—she's the one over there—we'd be honored."

Ken cleared his throat. "That's really nice of you. The thing is, I just have a day or so in the city, and I haven't seen my folks in almost a year."

"Oh, sure, I understand," the girl said. "No problem. Anyhow, if you ever have more time, this is our number. I'm Cheryl, and my friend's Dana." She walked off, her behind wiggling in her jeans.

When we got off the subway, Ken looked at me and laughed. "Wow. Have I changed, or is it New York? Things like that never happened to me before."

"It never happened to *me*," I said.

"Maybe it's my beard," he said. "Some women have this thing about men with beards. Either they hate it, or they love it. There doesn't seem to be any middle ground. She was pretty cute. Maybe *you* should look her up, Pete."

"No," I said quickly. "She wasn't my type."

"What's your type?" he said in an amused older-brother way.

"I'm not sure," I said, embarrassed.

Aline and Dad had a dinner party to go to that night, so Leslie, Ken, and I went out to a pizza place near the house. When we came back home, I brought some new records into the living room and played them for Ken. He always used to share his records with me before he went away to school and even gave me quite a few.

"This is the one Peter and I like the best," Leslie said. She'd been pretty quiet all evening, mostly listening to Ken tell us about his trip.

"I wish I had more time to get to know you, Leslie," Ken said. "Maybe you and Peter can come out to Chicago and visit."

"I might go to college there," Leslie said. She told him about the other places she'd applied to. Then, almost without thinking, she lay down on the couch and put her feet in my lap. Normally I'd have wanted to touch or caress them, but with Ken there, I felt too ill at ease to do anything. "Did Peter say anything?" she asked Ken after a moment.

"About what?"

There was a second's pause.

"He told me about getting early admission to Harvard," Ken said.

"Yeah, right," Leslie said. Her feet were wiggling in my lap like fish.

"Is that what you meant?" Ken looked from me to Leslie.

"I meant more about our sleeping together," Leslie said.

"No, I didn't know about that," Ken said calmly.

"It started last summer," Leslie said. "It has nothing to do with . . . We feel strange about it, even though we're not doing anything wrong." She looked at me. "Why aren't you saying anything?"

I felt like killing Leslie. It's one thing for her to talk to Mira about us, but Ken is my brother. If anyone ought to tell him, it's me.

"I'm glad," Ken said. "Though I can see it could be tricky."

"Peter, why aren't you saying anything?" Leslie repeated, her voice rising.

"What should I say?"

"Are you mad again?" She turned to Ken. "I guess I wasn't supposed to tell you. He thinks no one should know. I don't get that. I've told two people, that's all. Mira, my best friend, and you . . . because you seem sympathetic."

"I'm glad you told me," Ken said.

"I hate it when you do this," Leslie said to me, pulling her feet off my lap. "I really *hate* it."

"Do what?" I said quietly.

"He has this moral superiority thing," Leslie said to Ken. "Like he's this great perfect genius, and everyone else, we're all just little, hopeless worms crawling around in the mud at his feet."

"I think Peter's a very private person," Ken said. "He doesn't—"

"But you're his brother!" Leslie exclaimed. "Why *shouldn't* you know?"

"Maybe he felt he wanted to tell me himself," Ken suggested gently.

"Was that it?" Leslie asked me. "Were you planning on telling him yourself?"

I shrugged.

"We're extremely unsuited to each other," Leslie said. "There are times like now when I *hate* him! And then suddenly he'll be nice. I can't figure it out."

"If you love someone, it can get pretty intense," Ken said. He told her about Samantha. He brought out some photos he'd taken of her and her three sons. "She's the first person I've ever felt this strongly about."

"You seem so open," Leslie said admiringly. "How come you and Peter are so different?"

"We're not," Ken said. "We're a lot alike actually."

I was surprised at his saying that and flattered. Suddenly I realized I'd been acting stupid. Maybe Leslie was right. It wasn't that I felt like giving a press conference or telling Mom and Dad, but I was glad she'd told Ken. Reaching out, I put my arm lightly around the back of the couch, not quite touching her. I was afraid she'd jerk away, but she leaned back so my hand touched her neck. Then she put her hand over mine.

"More than anything, we're friends," Leslie said. "We can tell each other anything. I never had that with a boy before."

"I guess I still feel worried," I said, holding her hand tighter, entwining our fingers, "about Dad or Leslie's mother finding out."

Ken smiled. "I wouldn't worry. I think they're too wrapped up in each other to notice a whole lot."

Leslie leaned forward. "Do you think they love each other? What do you think?"

"Sure." Then he added, "I never can tell anything about what Dad feels. He's pretty distant with us."

"I think he likes me," Leslie said and then blushed. "Maybe he likes girls better. Maybe he should've had daughters."

Even though we talked about other things the rest of the evening, I felt good that Ken knew about us and accepted it so easily.

The next morning, since Ken wasn't leaving until after breakfast, Dad had gone out and gotten some bagels, smoked fish, and cream cheese. I exercised admirable restraint, considering those are among my favorite foods.

"Where will you be staying?" Dad asked Ken. "Does your roommate still have a place for you?"

"He graduated," Ken said. "No, actually, I met someone while I was traveling, and they offered to put me up for a while."

"Another student?" Dad pursued.

"No, she *was* a student. Now she's working as a piano tuner."

Dad laughed. "That's a means of support?"

"She gets some child support money from her ex-husband," Ken said, looking embarrassed.

"Where are her children?" Aline asked.

"They live with her, but it's a big house. I'll have my own room."

"I should hope so," Dad said. "It sounds like a peculiar kind of arrangement. What are the advantages?"

I guess because Ken had told us all about Samantha, I knew how awkward he must be feeling, but he covered it pretty well. "Well, like I say, it's a big house, and I like her kids. They're three boys. I told her I'd help out with them some afternoons in exchange for a cut on the rent."

"Won't that interfere with your studies?" Dad said. "After all, you've taken a year off. It'll be hard enough getting back in the saddle."

"How old is she?" Aline asked.

"Samantha?" Ken looked nervous. He put a slice of smoked salmon back.

"The woman you'll be renting from."

"Uh, I believe somewhere in her early thirties or thereabouts."

"Is she involved with anyone?" Aline went on.

Ken hesitated. "Yes . . . I think she is."

Dad shook his head. "Ken, I hate to say this, but it sounds like a really dopey idea. A divorcée with three kids and a lover? Can't you find a better set up than that? Those women are hardly the most stable—"

"What do you mean?" Aline broke in. "Why shouldn't she be stable just because she's divorced?"

"I don't mean it that way," Dad said. "I just meant that if she's trying to nail down another man and raise three kids plus doing a bit of piano tuning on the side—"

"Dad, piano tuning is her profession, okay?" Ken said, clearly trying not to explode.

"And why do you say 'nailing down' another man?" Aline said. "She's involved with someone! What does that have to do with nailing anyone down?"

It was great seeing both of them lash into Dad. I looked over at Leslie, who was hunched over, trying not to laugh.

"Look, darling, I have nothing against divorced women, but most of them, till they get a replacement, are full of bitterness and rage and ready to pounce on anyone who passes by. You may *think* you're safe, Ken, just because she's an older woman, quote unquote, but, believe me, those women are *dangerous*. You can't tell what might happen."

By now I could see Ken was furious. "Dad, will you stay the fuck out of my personal life? Is yours so great that you're in a position to give advice? Samantha happens to be one of the finest, most sensitive human beings it's been my privilege to meet. I'm honored that she's willing to let me stay with her."

Dad threw up his hands. "Advice withdrawn. What are you smirking about, Leslie? Is there something funny about this that I don't get?"

"No," Leslie shot back. "I just don't see what's wrong with older women and younger men. You fall in love with a person, not an age."

"Okay, but take it from me, at a certain age a man wants a woman who'll make *him* feel younger, not some graying, overweight dame who reminds him of his mother."

"How can you *be* so sexist?" Leslie said. *"Dame?"*

But Aline was even more upset. "I agree. My goodness, what a stereotype, Nelson! Since when are all older women graying and out of shape? Besides, Ken is *rooming* with this woman, not making love to her."

There was a pause.

"Well, I make love to her too, actually," Ken said wryly.

Dad sighed. "Amen. I rest my case."

"You don't *have* a case!" Aline said. "You just have a set of outworn, absurd, cruel ideas, and I think it's wonderful your sons don't share them." With that she got up and left the room.

I glanced over at Dad. He looked the way I sometimes feel when Leslie flares up at me. "Women," he sighed, appealing to me and Ken.

Neither of us said anything.

"Yes, we're such mysterious, complex, unfathomable little creatures, aren't we?" Leslie said. "Who knows what we'll do next."

"Look at me," Dad said, appealing to the three of us. "Aline is my age, give or take a year or two. I wasn't talking about *all* women. Naturally there are some women who make an effort to stay in shape, and it works to their advantage. But these are the exceptions."

"Boo! Hiss!" Leslie yelled, throwing a bagel at him. "You're an absolute menace! I don't know if I should even play squash with you again."

Dad folded his hands in a praying position. "Please, Les, not that. I'll reform. I'm a good guy. I *love* women . . . older women, younger women. Ask anyone."

"Who should I ask?" Leslie said playfully, looking at him sideways.

What infuriated me was the way she was flirting with him.

"It's important for everyone to be in shape," Dad went on, "not *just* women. Look at Peter. If he got in shape, maybe—"

"He has large bones," Leslie said, looking at me just as I was reaching for another bagel. "He's in excellent shape for his body structure."

"Les, I'm not in excellent shape," I said.

She ignored me. "I know lots of girls who find Peter *extremely* sexy," she said to Dad. "Mira said she'd be terribly happy if someday she was lucky enough to find someone as unique and intelligent and sensitive as Peter."

Dad laughed. "Well! I seem to be defeated on all fronts. Apologies to everyone! And, Ken, if you want to make that plane, you'd better step on it."

We promised Ken we'd keep in touch. "You were good," he said to Leslie as we waited in the lobby for the doorman to get a cab. "Maybe it's easier for you since he's not your father, but keep at him. Maybe he'll reform."

"I will," Leslie said. We were holding hands as Ken's cab drove off. "Thanks for defending me," I said as we turned back into the building.

"You should defend yourself," Leslie said. "He's so awful!"

"Then why do you flirt with him?"

"Flirt with your *father*? You're crazy! How was I flirting?"

"Your whole manner—arch, flip, throwing bagels . . ." I imitated her.

Leslie dropped my hand. "I'll tell you one thing: I'm never going to sleep with you again," she said. "Just leave me alone."

I saw the doorman glance at us. "I'll call Mira," I said, trying to be jocular.

"Do that," Leslie said. "And I'll go off and fuck your father, okay?"

The elevator door opened on that remark, and two middle-aged women walked out and stared at me. Leslie didn't speak to me for the rest of the day.

PART IV

Where To Draw the Line

LOOK, WE FOUGHT THE GOOD FIGHT," NELSON SAID. "WE have nothing to be ashamed of." He was still out of breath and handed me the small towel with which he'd been wiping the perspiration off his brow.

We'd gotten through the first two rounds of the father-daughter squash competition and then been eliminated by a small wiry team who were incredibly quick. "They're favored to win," Nelson said. "They've won for the past two years. I was hoping we could avoid them till the last round."

"I think we did well," I said. "Considering I just learned to play two months ago."

"You were super," Nelson said cheerfully. "You're a real trouper. I hope you keep on with it at college."

"I want to."

Just then I saw Nelson wave at a woman who was up in the gallery watching the other games which were going on simultaneously. She came down the aisle and went with us to the hallway outside the shower room. "I guess you were out of your league," she said. She was tall and pretty with brown hair in a ponytail.

"Leslie, this is Monica. She's directed me on a few commercials," Nelson said. "My stepdaughter, Leslie."

"Hi," I said. "I didn't know they had women directors for TV."

"They don't much," Monica said. "But a few places are willing to give you a try. It's hard to know where it will lead, though. I'd really like to do features someday."

"She's terrific," Nelson said. "The best. Someday she'll be a major director."

Monica looked pleased. "Hey, thanks. Your father's not so bad himself. I made him repeat one line forty times, and he finally did it perfectly."

"She works us to death," Nelson said with a mock pout. "If she wasn't so pretty . . ."

He and Monica grinned at each other. "So call me," she said. "I *think* Wednesday's fine, but there may be a problem."

"Will do," he said.

As I showered, I thought of Mom sitting in front of her three-way mirror the other day pulling back the skin around her eyes and saying, "I wish I didn't think facelifts were immoral." I remembered the fights she and Nelson had been having, and I felt a pang at the thought that something might be going on between Nelson and Monica, who looked so fresh and spirited and feisty.

Nelson and I had an orange drink after we showered. I wouldn't have brought Monica up again, but he said, "And she's a terrific squash player too. Just like you, Les, quick, intense, competitive."

"I always thought you didn't like competitiveness in women."

"No, I think it's wonderful. I've always liked women who were out in the world making the most of themselves, looking good, fighting hard. Where would they be if they didn't?"

"Does she have a boyfriend?" I pulled an ice cube out of my drink and crunched on it.

"Who?"

"Monica."

"Well, I'm sure she . . . She's extremely attractive. I'm sure many men . . . But I don't think she has anyone." He cleared his throat. "She'd have to answer that."

I felt like everything in the room was very bright and very sharp. "I don't want Mom to get hurt," I said, looking at the wall.

Nelson didn't answer for a moment. "No, of course not," he said.

"Please don't do anything to hurt her," I added, my heart thumping painfully.

Nelson was looking down into his drink. "I'm not that kind of person," he said. "I've always been very discreet. I—"

"Meaning if she doesn't know, it doesn't matter?"

His face hardened. "Meaning it's none of your business! I'm very fond of you, Leslie, you know that, but I feel you should realize my relationship with Aline is between us. You have your own life to figure out."

"She's my mother," I said shakily. "It would be awful if you cheated on her, whether she knew or not. And she'd know! And if you're doing it right now with that Monica, you should be ashamed! Horribly ashamed!"

He just stared at me. "Is that the end of that?"

"Yes!"

What really bothers me is that I feel there's some kind of undercurrent between me and Nelson—even when we fight.

Maybe he's just the kind of man that many women respond to, and he responds back, not having any particular intentions. But I hated the way the scene had ended with his having the upper hand.

I don't know if it was because of that, but the next day, when I had to play a very tense, emotional scene in *The Barretts* where Mel keeps grilling me about my relationship with my "lover," I ended up bursting into tears. The father Mel plays isn't like Nelson *or* like Daddy. He's very much a Victorian father, removed, stern, puritanical, but I had the same sense that I have at times with both of them that there was no way I could reach him.

Afterward I pulled myself together and rushed off stage. Mira came over and hugged me. "That was super," she said. "But are you okay?"

"I don't know." I still felt shaky. "Could I come to your house?" I asked. "Maybe sleep over?"

"Of course." Mira looked taken aback at my plaintiveness. "Are you really okay?"

"Sure. It's only that I don't want to go home right now." I couldn't face Mom and Nelson just then.

When Mira and her mother are getting along, I love going there. It's so much more informal and relaxed than at our house. She and her mother act like sisters, teasing each other, yelling, but it's never tense.

"So what's with Peter?" Mira asked as we were having coffee in her room. "You haven't mentioned him lately."

"I don't know," I said. "It seems like he's always at the lab. Sometimes I think he's a really neurotic person."

"Who isn't?" Mira asked.

"Everything is wrong at home lately," I said. "Mom and Nelson have fights, Peter and his father hate each other. . . ."

"But what about the two of you?"

"That's not too good either. Sometimes I think all Peter

really cares about is science. Maybe I'm just an experiment for him." I knew I was letting myself sink into an orgy of despair and self-pity, but I couldn't stop myself.

Mira sighed. "He did seem kind of detached . . . but not mean. I got the feeling he really cared for you."

"But if it's someone you're sleeping with, it hurts when they act like that," I said. "I look up at meals, and he's sitting there observing me, 'studying' me. Is *he* so terrific? He never had a girl friend before. He should be grateful I like him!"

"I think he is," Mira suggested. "That's just his character. He can't help it."

"Yeah, but why?" I burst out. "Why are men always like that?"

Mira laughed. "I should know? Listen, it's just the way it is. Maybe it's that their sex organs hang outside their bodies. Maybe it's that we connect sex with the possibility of getting pregnant. I don't know. It's a bitch. If you're not gay, you just have to find a way around it, find men who deep down are caring, even if they don't show it that well. I think Peter's one of those."

"Yeah?" I felt she was right. You have to read between the lines so much with men. If only it could be direct and open the way it is when Mira and I talk together.

Usually talking to Mira makes me feel better, but this time, after the lights were out, I just lay there, unable to sleep, suddenly anxious about the play. The performance is in six weeks and Peter and Mom and Nelson will all be coming, to say nothing of Peter's mother and her friend Muriel. I'd really pay to have all of them stay away. Of course I won't see them, but knowing they're in the audience will make it tricky.

When I saw Daddy the next week, I said, "I wish in a way I could live with you."

He leaned forward. "Is it really so bad? What's been going on?"

In the past, when my parents were still married to each other, I felt Daddy and I could discuss just about everything. Partly that was because if there was a scene with Mom or a bad patch between us, he was there, he knew. But I've been reluctant to mention anything about the tension that exists now. It seems unfair to get Daddy involved in the complications of Mom's new marriage just as he's setting up a life without her. It's my problem now, not his.

I decided to try to talk to him instead—obliquely—about Peter.

"I've been seeing this boy," I said, "and it isn't going well."

"A boy from school?"

"Yes."

"Is he in the play with you?"

"Yes."

"Well, that is difficult, seeing him every day. I remember once having a relationship with a woman in my building when I was fresh out of college, and after we broke up, I saw her twice a day in the elevator or the lobby. It was agony."

I wonder how Daddy would feel if he knew Mom and Nelson were having problems. He isn't a vindictive person. Still, I didn't want to say anything. "Nelson and I entered the father-daughter squash competition," I said. "We lost in the third round."

"I feel insanely jealous. He must be in wonderful shape."

"Fair. He thinks he's better than he is."

"That's probably a secret to success," Daddy said. "Knowing one's limits may be the first step to wisdom and maturity, but it can sure be a drag."

* * *

As I walked in the door at home, Mom ran out, waving two letters. I could see one was from Chicago and one from Wesleyan. "I haven't opened them," she said. "I swear."

I took them into my room, closed the door, and tried to decide which to open first. Since I care more about Chicago, I opened the Wesleyan one first. I'd gotten on their waiting list. Then, with my eyes closed, I opened the Chicago one. I'd gotten in! Without even thinking I tore out and hugged Mom. "I'm in!" I said.

She took the letters from me, read them, and then looked up with a really pleased smile. "I'm so glad, Les. I knew you'd get in."

"My SAT scores were so rotten, I was afraid they'd hold that against me, but I guess they didn't."

"They weren't rotten," Mom said. "Didn't you get in the six hundreds in English?"

"I must have been a borderline case."

"We should celebrate," Mom said. "Let me see if we have any champagne."

Usually we eat at seven thirty, but Nelson wasn't home, so Mom said we should start without him.

"Where is he?" I asked.

"Probably working late," Mom said. Her eyes connected with mine, and then she looked away.

Peter seemed somewhere in outer space during dinner. He said it was great I'd gotten into Chicago, drank one glass of champagne, and then told us he was going to skip dessert because he had some reading to do.

Mom and I had dessert alone. "I suppose after getting into Harvard, Chicago doesn't seem like such a big deal," I said wryly.

"He's like his father," Mom said. "He's just moody."

I really don't think Peter is at all like Nelson, but I didn't say anything.

"Maybe he should have gone to Chicago with Hope this

winter," Mom said. "I don't blame you, Les, but you're so involved with school and your friends and the play. He seems so lonely. All he does is go to the lab or sit in his room."

"Well, that's his personality," I said, feeling the champagne go up my nose.

"Nelson isn't any help," Mom went on. "I don't think he really likes any of his sons, except to talk about when they're not around. Then you'd think he adored them."

"I think Peter'll be okay," I said.

"Sure he will," Mom said. "It's an awkward, painful stage. I wouldn't go through it again for the world. You at least have your acting. When I was seventeen, I just whirled from thing to thing, doing whatever I thought my parents wanted."

In photos when she was my age Mom always looks so cute and perky and self-confident. "You had lots of boyfriends, though, didn't you?" I said.

"Only in the most superficial way. Sex was verboten, so it was just endless scuffles over where to draw the line. And none of us ever thought of really trying to talk with a boy. For all our desire to get married as soon as we could, I think we thought of them as the enemy."

"Aren't they?" I said.

Mom laughed. "Today's not a good day to ask me." She looked at the kitchen clock. "Where is Nelson? Did he say anything to you this morning?"

"No, I didn't see him."

"He's such a contradiction," Mom said. "He adores women, so he says, but I wonder if he's ever in his life been faithful to anyone for more than one second. And each new woman thinks she'll have the magic that'll make him reform."

I had drunk the champagne a little too quickly; my face felt flushed. "Are you sorry you married him?"

Mom's face got a blank, sad expression. "I was abysmally naïve! We seemed to get along so well. I just don't know. . . ."

We sat in silence sipping our champagne. A few minutes later Nelson breezed in. "Listen, I'm really sorry," he said. "I called an hour or so ago, but the line was busy."

Mom just looked at him.

"The director was driving us all crazy, making us do take after take. She's really off the wall. Monica—you met her, Leslie, at the squash club. I'm all for women's rights, but . . ." He noticed the champagne. "Hey, what's the celebration?"

"I got into the University of Chicago," I said quietly.

He grabbed me and lifted me off the ground, kissing me. "That's my girl! Wonderful! Any left for me?" He held up the bottle.

"The fizz may have gone out of it," Mom said dryly.

Nelson poured himself a glass. "So? I'm a man who's easy to please. Fizz, no fizz." He held up his glass and clinked it against mine. "I'm really proud of you. I wish I could take the credit."

"It's not like getting into Harvard," I said.

"Oh, what's the difference?" Nelson said. "Chicago's just as good. Where's Peter? Does he know?"

"He's inside, working," Mom said. "We finished dinner half an hour ago."

Nelson kissed her on the forehead. "Darling, I am so sorry—I can't tell you. If it were up to me, that woman would be fired tomorrow and never allowed to work again. For one dinky three-minute commercial we rehearsed ten hours!"

"I don't see how you can say you called an hour ago," Mom said tensely. "We were eating then. No one was on the phone."

"Maybe I misdialed. I was frazzled beyond belief."

"Aren't you hungry?" The chicken was still out on the buffet.

"I had a bite on the set, a sandwich. . . . Ali, please don't go at me that way. I'm beat. I'm here, Leslie's just gotten into a terrific college. Let's be happy, like the happy family we are."

"To happy families," Mom said sarcastically, raising her empty glass.

Nelson looked at me. "Les, you believe me, don't you?"

I shrugged.

"What's *with* both of you? Have I been tried in absentia? Is this the Last Supper?"

"We think you've been off making it with other women," I said. "You were probably in bed with Monica, not on the set with her."

Nelson turned red.

"Leslie, that's enough," Mom said sharply. "You have no right to say something like that. Please apologize."

I looked at her in bewilderment. "To who? For what?"

"I'm perfectly capable of fighting my own battles," Mom said. "You're being childish and absurd."

"Well, I'm moving to Daddy's," I said, jumping up. "I'll let the two of you be 'happy' all by yourselves."

I went into my room, threw some clothes in a suitcase, and went to the bathroom for my toothbrush. Peter peered in. "Where're you going?"

"I'm moving in with Daddy. You can remain in the happy home."

He closed the door behind him. "What happened?"

"Nothing! I just don't want to live here. I don't like *your* father or *my* mother or—"

"How about me?" he said plaintively. "Can I go with you? I don't like them either."

"Peter, you've hardly said one word to me for two weeks! Why should you want to come with me?"

Suddenly he looked desperate. "Everything's horrible," he said. "I hate this year. You act lovely-dovey and then turn off for no reason. Nothing I do pleases anyone. It's no use!" He turned away, his back to me.

I've never heard Peter sound that way. He's usually so totally reserved and diffident. "It's being here. It's making both of us crazy," I said. "Come with me. Daddy can put both of us up."

His face still held that tormented look. "Do you really want me to come?"

"Yes."

We decided to wait till later, when Mom and Nelson were asleep. I put the suitcase in my closet and pretended to go to bed at ten, which is my usual bedtime. Mom and Nelson always turn in at eleven. At midnight Peter knocked very quietly on my door.

I came out with my suitcase, carrying my shoes so I wouldn't make much noise. We tiptoed down the hall and closed the door silently behind us. I put a note about where we were on the dining room table.

What I like about the doorman is that he never questions anything. When we asked him to get us a cab, he stepped outside and blew his whistle. He didn't seem to think there was anything strange about two teenagers leaving home with suitcases at twelve thirty at night.

In the cab Peter held my hand tightly. "I hope your father doesn't mind my coming too," he said.

"I'll tell him he has to have both of us. Otherwise—"

"Look, I have some money in the bank. If he won't take us, we can rent a place for two months."

"Could we?" I felt nervous at the thought of it. I still had school and exams and the play.

"You'd keep going to school," Peter said. Suddenly he was the way he usually is, practical, planning it all out. "We can find a place near the school."

"How about meals."

"I can cook. Can't you?"

"Sort of. But what if they come after us?"

Peter was stroking my hand. "Don't worry, Les. We'll find a way out of this."

Two for the Road

LESLIE'S FATHER WAS STILL UP WHEN WE ARRIVED AT HIS apartment. He didn't look that surprised at seeing the two of us, just listened to Leslie's explanation of why we had left. "If you won't let us stay here, we'll run away!" she said wildly. "We'll go to a hotel."

"Sweetie," Leslie's father said gently, "of course you can stay here. Don't be silly."

"Can Peter stay too?"

"Of course . . . if he doesn't mind using the sleep couch. How are you with sofa beds, Peter?"

"Fine," I said. "I can sleep on anything."

"But, Daddy, this is permanent. I mean, till we go to college, not just for tonight."

"I understand. And if it's all right with Aline, it's fine with me." He cleared his throat. "She knows you're here?"

Leslie looked at me. "Well, she'll know in the morning. We left a note."

Leslie's father was silent. "In other words she doesn't know now?"

"She's asleep. . . . Daddy, it's just too upsetting, listening to them go at each other and then her blaming me no matter which side I take."

"I understand that," Leslie's father said, "but legally she's got custody. I can't simply take you in, either of you, without going to court."

"Then we'll go to a hotel, or rent our own place. We're *not* going back there!"

Leslie's father looked at me. "Do you feel the same way, Peter? Has it been as unpleasant for you?"

"I want to be with Leslie," I said cautiously.

"I see," Leslie's father said. I wasn't sure what he saw. "Well, look, let's get to sleep, and in the morning I'll speak to Aline and see if some solution can't be found. We don't want the two of you roaming about the city on your own. You deserve a quiet place to live till you graduate."

At that Leslie threw herself into her father's arms and started sobbing. I couldn't hear most of what she said, but he patted her back and murmured comforting things. I felt a pang of jealousy. "Everything's going to be fine," he said. "Don't worry, puss. I'll take care of it."

In the morning Leslie's father said he thought Leslie should go to school. He'd gotten up early, at seven, when we did. She left looking subdued and tired.

About half an hour after she left, her mother called. I was in the kitchen fixing some cereal. I heard Leslie's father saying, "No, she left for school. Of course, I didn't, I had no idea. It was a total surprise to me. . . . I have *not* kidnaped them! They left of their own free will, and I simply want them to be somewhere peaceful and quiet where they can . . . Of course! Lunch is fine." For the rest of the conversation he mostly listened. When he hung up, he looked at me and sighed. "Well, I don't know. This may be more complex than Leslie is aware." He poured himself some coffee in a large flowered mug. "Did you . . . uh, how long have you been considering this move?"

I told him I had never thought of it at all. "But when Leslie seemed so upset, I didn't want her to just go off alone."

"That was thoughtful of you," he said. "Thank you, Peter. Leslie does things a bit impulsively at times. I feel you've had a good influence on her."

"I—I love her," I stammered.

"Yes, of course. I'm glad. She's never had that kind of closeness with a boy. Perhaps if she'd had an actual brother . . ."

I couldn't tell if he was willfully misunderstanding me or not, but it was a relief. I hadn't meant to blurt that out. I got dressed and told Leslie's father I was going to the lab. But instead I spent the day by myself, walking about the city. It was a mild April day in the sixties, good for walking. I went through the park, had lunch sitting under a tree, and then bought a paper and looked to see if any good old movies were playing. In some ways I wish Leslie and I could rent a place by ourselves. I imagined the two of us together every night, talking, working, seeing movies, making love. But I wonder if Leslie would really do that. She's impulsive, but she's also a coward in a lot of ways. Maybe it's because she's an only child, but when she flung herself into her father's arms the night before, assuming he could handle everything for her, she reminded me of a little girl. Maybe when I was seven or eight, I had those kinds of illusions about my parents, but they're certainly long gone by now.

I ended up seeing a movie called *Two for the Road* with Audrey Hepburn and Albert Finney. They were a couple who met when they were young and had a kid; both of them were unfaithful, but they still seemed to be together at the end. It kept jumping around in time, and the only way you could tell what decade the characters were in was by the fashions and the hairdos. When it was over, there was a break. I went to the lobby to get some popcorn and a soda. There was a girl standing at the soda machine. "This is the fourteenth time I've seen this," she said.

"It's my first time." I searched in my pockets for some quarters.

"I'm a Audrey Hepburn freak," she said. "I love old movies. Like, today I should be at school, but it was such a gorgeous day, and I figured what the heck."

"What school do you go to?" I asked. She was nice-looking and seemed friendly.

"Windsor School for Girls. It's in Riverdale."

"Do you know someone named Leslie Hertz?"

"Yeah, isn't she the one who acts?"

"She's my stepsister."

"Huh . . . Do you go to the Windsor School for Boys?"

"I graduated in January."

"Leslie's a really good actress," she said as I put in my dimes for soda. "Do you act too? By the way, I'm Karen Ludowsky."

"I'm Peter," I said after a moment's hesitation.

Karen followed me down the aisle. When I got to my seat, she looked at the seat next to it. It was empty. "Would you mind if I joined you?" she asked. "I came in when it had already started, and there's this woman with a huge hairdo in front of me."

"It's fine with me," I said. Karen looked younger than me, maybe fifteen or sixteen. She had a nice figure and straight black hair, not as pretty as Leslie, but reasonable.

The next movie was *A Little Romance*, which I doubt I would have liked much had I actually watched it. It was about two kids loose in France and Italy. The girl, Diane

Lane, was outstandingly pretty and had a screwy mother. Laurence Olivier appeared from time to time and said wise and bemused things. There may have been a plot, but not so as you'd notice. What happened was that right in the middle of the opening credits Karen tugged on my sleeve. "Want to share my popcorn?"

"Sure." As I was about to reach for it, she took a handful and put it piece by piece into my mouth, like I was an animal at the zoo. Then she kissed me very lightly. "You taste salty."

In the movies I always feel I'm a different person. The dark, the big faces looming up, all those dramatic, incredible lives pulling you into theirs. I mean, I'm not schizo. I know I'm just me, Peter, watching a movie, but I feel looser, more expansive, happier. Maybe that was why I started making out with Karen, whom I didn't know and whom I'm pretty positive wouldn't have liked me if she knew me. I felt as though it were the most natural thing in the world, as though I did it every time I went to the movies instead of sitting there hunched up, embroiled in a million fantasies. We kissed forever, and she even let me put my hand under her sweater and touch her breasts. Thank God no one was behind us! In fact, the theater was almost empty. In between kisses Karen would take a deep breath and say, "Oh, wait, this is one of my favorite parts," wolf down some popcorn, and then turn back to me.

When the lights came on at the end, she smiled. "I still like it. I've seen it ten times. After Audrey Hepburn, Laurence Olivier is my favorite, just in terms of pure acting. Did you ever see *Wuthering Heights*?"

"Yeah." I was trying to recover from the feelings that making out had stirred up, not just excitement but some kind of guilt.

"That's what I want, what Cathy had with Heathcliff, total all-out passion, where you and the other person are the same person. Do you know what I mean?"

"I don't think I'd want anything quite that extreme," I said.

She shook her head and got up, her coat over her arm. "Yeah, boys never do," she said. "That's the trouble. Mom says I'll get over it. She says wanting to blend totally is immature. It has to be you *plus* someone else."

All I could think of was Leslie and her reaction if she knew what had happened. "Um . . . Could you not tell Leslie about this?" I said. "It's just that she—"

"Oh, sure," Karen said. "I know! She thinks because you're her brother, you've never heard of sex or anything. My older brother's just like that. He thinks I'm still lying under the piano trying to get Barbi and Ken together."

"Is she in your class?" I put my coat on. It was twilight, raining slightly, turning gray.

"No, I'm just a sophomore . . . Well, take care. See you around!"

If this had been any other time in my life, I would have asked for her phone number, but there was no way I could do that without getting into trouble. Still, I felt incredibly good. It's strange with girls. I wonder if this is going to be a pattern in my life. The few times I've tried to get anywhere with someone, it hasn't worked at all, but with Leslie and this time with Karen it seems like they were just attracted to me for no reason I can figure out. Sheer animal magnetism, I guess.

I look better. I really think I do. Maybe I've dropped a few pounds, but whatever it is, I don't cringe so much when I pass a mirror. Walking home from the movie, I thought: *I'll have other girls in college if I want them. This is just the beginning*. I felt a pang of guilt even thinking that, but at the same time the knowledge of it flickered through me, like someone's hand caressing me.

I rang Leslie's father's doorbell. Leslie answered. She still looked upset. "Where were you? I tried the lab, and they said you hadn't been in."

"I couldn't face it," I said. "I went to the movies."

"Well, you have to go back," she said. "Daddy met with Mom at lunch, and she says I can stay here, but she sees no reason you should too."

"Shit." I hated the idea of returning there by myself with Dad and Aline hovering over me. When would I see Leslie? "Why don't we go off by ourselves like I said? I can swing it financially. It would be great. Let's do it!" I felt buoyed up by the movie and the sexual excitement of a stranger suddenly wanting me, if only temporarily.

"I told Daddy about that," Leslie said. "He says he could get in terrible trouble. Mom would think he put us up to it."

I grabbed her hands. "But would you want to do it?"

She still looked hesitant. "Sure, in a way, but . . . Well, it would be almost like living together, and we're so young. I don't know if I'm ready for that."

I hate it when Leslie does her little girl bit. "Sure, okay, I get it." I turned away angrily.

"I mean, part of me would love to," Leslie said in a soft voice. "But there's the play, final exams. I can't just drop everything and concentrate on you! There's more to my *life* than that!"

"There's more to *my* life too," I said. "I just want something to hang on to, something solid. This whole year everything seems to be falling apart at the seams. At least what we have is real."

"Is it?"

"What do you mean? Of course it is. Why do you do that, Les? Isn't it real for you?"

"Daddy thinks I'm awfully young to . . . make that kind of commitment," Leslie said.

That stopped me short. "How does he know? You didn't tell *him* too, did you?"

"Not everything. I had to tell him something, Peter! How

would it make sense otherwise, your coming with me? I just said we cared about each other a lot."

I laughed bitterly. "God, who *doesn't* know now? It's getting to be ridiculous!"

Leslie put her hand on my neck. "He doesn't know we—"

"What's between us is private, or ought to be. You trivialize it by telling everyone. You make it into a joke."

Leslie's voice was trembling. "I don't see how you can say that. I love you more than anyone. I just don't want to get sucked in, see the whole year, everything I've worked for, crumble."

I put my arms around her. "Les, it won't. You won't let it. I just want to see you more than once a week."

"You're seeing me now."

"Where's your father?"

"He went to get some stuff for supper. He promised Mom you'd be back tonight."

The lights were still off in the living room. Leslie sat down next to me on the couch, and we began kissing in a hungry, nervous way, knowing her father could come back at any minute. "I wish we could be together tonight," I whispered. "I'll call Dad and tell him I'll be back tomorrow."

"Okay," Leslie said limply, seeming dazed. "That's a good idea."

All through dinner I tried to look at Leslie and think of our being in bed together. I'd try to think of something else and Karen would pop into my mind, that strange, unexpected moment when she began putting the popcorn in my mouth, the funny pungent scent of some cologne she was wearing, her bare foot wriggling against my leg as though it had an identity of its own.

"I'm sorry, Peter," Leslie's father said. "I tried my best. But it's true, just in terms of room, my place would be a little small for the two of you. Not that I'd mind, but . . ."

"Sure, I understand." What would he think if he knew about us? Not just that we "cared for each other a lot," but that we were sleeping together? Leslie's father is so ironical and held back that it's impossible to imagine what he feels, except how much he loves Leslie.

"You can come over weekends, of course. Feel free to do that any time."

After dinner Leslie said she felt tired and wanted to go to bed. I pretended I did too and went into the living room to set up the sleep couch. I'd hoped Leslie's father might turn in too, but for two more hours I heard him puttering around in the kitchen. Every time there'd be five minutes of silence and I'd think he'd finally turned in, he'd give a cough or turn on some music on the radio. It got to be past midnight. I was afraid Leslie might be asleep. For myself I felt too wired up to sleep, even though I hadn't slept much the night before. Finally, after there'd been a patch of silence that went on for ten minutes, I got up and padded out into the hall. Leslie's father was just coming out of the bathroom. He was in his pajamas. He raised his hand in a salute and stepped aside to let me in. I stayed there a little while, flushed the toilet, and went back to bed. But this time I didn't climb in and lie down. I sat on the edge of the sleep couch, waiting. I watched the luminous numbers on the digital clock. When it said 12:45, I went in.

I opened Leslie's door as softly as I could and then closed it behind me. She half sat up. "Peter?" she whispered.

I took my clothes off and slipped into bed with her. "It's the Masked Marvel," I said.

"You don't have anything on!" she said, as though I had forgotten my pajamas by mistake.

"That's right, I don't, do I? You seem a bit overclad yourself." I tried unbuttoning her pajama top.

"I'm cold," she said, shivering, burrowing against me. "I thought you'd never come."

"I was waiting for your father to turn in. He didn't go to bed till fifteen minutes ago."

"I know. I heard him. Should I take everything off?"

"Can't hurt. I'll keep you warm."

Leslie sat up and pulled off her pajama bottoms. "It's the end of my period—is that okay? I think it's almost over."

"Sure. But why don't we get a towel, just in case? Blood-stained sheets might look a little suspicious."

"It's really *over,*" Leslie said, but I got a towel from the bathroom anyway and placed it over the sheet.

I think, for all my need to make love to Leslie right then in her father's apartment, I felt nervous too. Leslie clung to me in a way that seemed childlike rather than sexual, making very soft sounds at the end, like a kitten when you step on its tail. As she lay in my arms afterward, I thought of the fantasied apartment, the two of us together, no parents, no rules. I wondered if someone more forceful than me might've convinced Leslie to do it. Or would've just gone out and rented a place and taken her there, as though it were settled. A montage of pictures crossed my mind, like those in the movie I'd seen: Leslie and me having dinner, Leslie sitting on my lap, reading, our showering together, her trimming my toenails.

"Thanks for leaving Mom's with me last night," she said finally. "I don't know if I'd have had the courage by myself."

"Sure you would."

"I'm a terrible coward," Leslie said. "I'm not like you. You just do what you want. You don't care so much what other people think. I always care."

"I care too," I said, a little reluctant to spoil her image of me.

"I wish I was independent enough to do what you said, just have us live together, but I'm not."

I wondered whether it was because if we were together,

we could make love whenever we wanted, if that was something Leslie feared. I asked her, trying to phrase it as tentatively as possible.

"I just don't want to be gobbled up!" she exclaimed. "I don't *want* that! I want to be me, not just part of you."

I thought of what Karen had said at the movies about *Wuthering Heights*. "You're you, I'm me," I joked.

"But when we're together, I feel . . . I don't know, as though I was blurring, as though I was *less* me. Do you understand?"

"Sort of." We lay there together, and after a while Leslie fell asleep. I heard her breathing change and become deeper and more regular. I didn't want to fall asleep in her bed, so I disentangled myself, put my pajamas back on, and went out into the living room.

It was past two. But even though I didn't feel wired up in quite the same way, I still couldn't fall asleep. I lay there till dawn, watching the light patterns on the ceiling, hearing sounds outside from cars, people yelling, all the night sounds of the city.

Dream Of Success

IT'S BEEN THREE WEEKS SINCE I LEFT ALINE AND NELSON. Mostly I've been focused on the play. We've rehearsed the last scene of *The Barretts* so many times! I rerun it in my head all day long. I have the last line in the play, which Brandemour claims is crucial. It's just after the family has discovered that Elizabeth has eloped with Browning to Italy. Her father gets hysterical with rage and says he wants to have Elizabeth's dog, Flush, destroyed in revenge. The last line, mine, is "In her letter to me Ba writes that she has taken Flush with her." Ba is Henrietta's nickname for Elizabeth.

After I had said the line a hundred times, never quite right, Brandemour stopped the play. "Look, kids, here's what's going on. This is a man with iron, *total* control over his family and *no* self-understanding. He's mad, in a way, in love with his daughter, who has finally up and left him. In his line about wanting to kill Flush, you have to *see* it, that finally the mask has dropped, and he'll do anything to get revenge. And, you, Leslie, are saying to him that he can't, that his power has been broken, that not only have Elizabeth and Flush escaped, you are all free . . . if you want to be. That's what the play is about—the way we imprison ourselves. All of these people are prisoners, Elizabeth through her self-imposed illness, all the sons, the daughters. What's to stop any of them from walking out at any time?"

"How could they support themselves?" Bryna asked, "the girls, I mean? Women couldn't work then. They weren't trained."

"Women worked," Brandemour said. "Women have *always* worked. And how about the sons? Are they any freer, for all their masculine training and so forth? They are free when they declare themselves to be free. And that's true of all of us too."

Of me? I have what I thought I wanted all along now, living peacefully with Daddy, no fights, a miniature married couple, just what Mom once accused me of wanting. But is that what I really want? Or am I just hiding behind Daddy because I don't feel ready to move in with Peter, and I don't think it's just the secrecy we've had to weave around us all year. Maybe it *is* cowardice or immaturity, as Peter says, or fear of sex—God knows what.

That night Peter was coming over for dinner. As Daddy and I were cooking, we talked about the play. "I don't want you ever to feel the way Barrett made Elizabeth feel," he said after we ran through the last scene together.

"I don't," I said, amazed. "You're the opposite of the father in the play."

"Not totally. I want to keep you, to have you all to myself. But don't let me—fight back, no matter what."

"Of course, I will," I said, really puzzled. "But I really don't see any connection, Daddy. I just don't."

Dinner was nice, relaxed, except for the fact that I knew

Peter wanted to stay over. It was Friday so there was no real reason he shouldn't, as long as Mom and Nelson knew. But at around eleven Daddy said he felt Peter ought to go. "It's wise to be scrupulous about all these little details," he said.

Peter looked furious. "That's ridiculous," he said. "They don't give a damn where I am. Weekends are free."

"Nothing's free," Daddy said, "as you may, alas, learn later in life. Everything has a price."

I couldn't tell if he knew the reason Peter wanted to stay over.

"Leslie and I want to be alone together," Peter said. He didn't look at me for confirmation.

"Of course you do," Daddy said. "A perfectly understandable desire, which I have no wish to impede in any way. But the feelings of others must be respected."

"What do *you* want?" Peter said, turning to me. "Do you want me to stay?"

"Well sure. I—I—" I stammered. "But if Daddy doesn't think it would be good—"

"Oh, fuck it," Peter said and stormed out of the apartment.

"Ah, the volatility of the young," Daddy said. "Would that one could recapture some of that intensity later on!"

It was a beautiful, warm May evening. Our apartment is on the second floor. I ran to the French windows and pushed them open. "Peter!" I called out. He was just leaving the building.

He looked up.

"Just one sec. I'll be right down." I turned to Daddy. "I'll be back. I just want to speak to him a minute."

It was so warm, I didn't need a jacket. I just ran down the stairs to where Peter was standing outside. "It's three weeks till graduation," I said. "Why does it matter so much?"

"What changes after graduation?" Peter said fiercely. "Will you suddenly be a different person?"

"No, but I'll be able to do what I want. We can go off together, spend the summer together."

He faced me with that scowling, intense look, like a rhino about to charge. "Will you? Do you swear it?"

I nodded, feeling frightened.

"No running back to Daddy?"

"I promise!"

We kissed. I could feel his body trembling. "God, Les, I want you so much," he whispered.

"Three weeks," I whispered back. "Just three weeks."

As I went upstairs I wondered if Daddy had been watching us out the window. But when I came in, he was in the kitchen tidying up, a baroque sonata on the radio. "I love this piece," he said. "Why did I never take up the oboe? It's such a splendid instrument."

Not a word about Peter, about what he really thought about him or about our relationship. Poor Mom, I thought. First Daddy, who never says a direct word, then Nelson, who's so responsive he can't keep his hands off any appealing woman who passes by.

The night of the play I decided not to have dinner, just a glass of milk. I'd read somewhere that it isn't good to eat before a performance, and that most actors, onstage, just pretend to eat if it's part of the action. Daddy was coming alone, and Peter was coming with his mother and Muriel. I didn't know about Mom. I hadn't spoken to her since I left.

What bothered me most about that last evening with Mom was the change—Mom and I had been sitting there, talking with such rapport, and then Nelson appeared, and the whole thing shattered. I felt that when I accused him of making it with another woman I only said what Mom was feeling, but maybe she wasn't ready to throw all that out in the open yet. Maybe I did it too crudely. I really spoke up because I identified so strongly with her, was so angry at him. But I think it's as she said: This is her battle, and it was humiliating for her to have me watch it, be a witness, see her vulnerability.

As Mira was doing my makeup, I wondered if I wanted Mom to come. I guess deep down I do. Having this rift between us go on for so long has been painful. But I had to put it out of my mind and focus on getting ready. Mira is a whiz at makeup. She puts it on heavily, but once you're under the lights, it all pales out. She also helped me with the hairpiece I have to wear. My hair's growing back, but not enough for a really Victorian look. I have two dresses to wear in the play. The first one I love: it's wine-red silk with a high neck and small buttons down the back. It makes my waist seem much smaller than it really is.

Mira stood back to survey the total effect. "Super. How do you feel?"

"Shaky."

"Well, Petra's throwing up. Let's hope she gets it all out before she goes on stage."

For performances Brandemour always wears the same black pantsuit with velvet lapels and a white carnation in her buttonhole. Maybe it's for our sakes, or maybe by the night of the performance she's beyond caring, but she does a total personality transformation also. Instead of being talkative and volatile, she speaks very calmly and soothingly; nothing seems to faze her. I saw her spoon-feeding Petra some Pepto Bismol. "Probably it *is* a placebo," she was saying, "but most things in life are. That doesn't stop them from working."

Seeing me, she patted my cheek. "Lovely, dear. Your hair's perfect. Beautiful dress."

I saw Bryna peeking out at the audience. She looked stately and elegant in her black dress. By now I think of Bryna as Elizabeth, or maybe it's just that I think of Elizabeth differently. She plays her very maternally and warmly. Next to her Vladimir looks young, and his passion seems a little childish. She looks at him with an indulgent, adoring expression but always with a kind of dignity. I'd have been different, maybe not as good. Certainly now it doesn't seem to matter.

"There's my parents," she said quietly. "Oh, I wish so much they hadn't come."

I peeked around next to her. I saw Peter, his mother, and Muriel in one row. A moment later Daddy came in and joined them in the row behind. But I couldn't find Mom and Nelson. It was hard to see every row, especially in the balcony, but I felt a pang. "I'm not sure my mother is here," I said. "I don't see her."

"Are you nervous?" Bryna asked. "I'm not. I feel more numb."

"Me too."

My first line is, "What are you laughing at, Ba?" It comes pretty soon into the first scene, so I stayed to stage left while Bryna did her opening scene with the maid and the doctor. Then I came running on, feeling my dress swish around me.

All during the first act I felt divided in two. I didn't slip, I think I was in character, but I felt that odd sensation of watching myself, which can be nerve-racking because it's so subtle and so hard to get rid of. Petra muffed a line in the second scene. She was supposed to end a speech with "You're only asked to be a bridesmaid, darling, not a bride," and then I come in with "Yes, I know, but of—it's so hard to explain." When she didn't say the line, I waited just a second and then said mine, whereupon she said *her* line, almost running over mine. Brandemour says sometimes that's okay, to give the feeling of real speech when people interrupt each other, but here it didn't make much sense. A second later we moved on, and I forgot about it.

After the first act it was terrific. By the time I got to the confrontation scene with Mel, I felt really good. And by the final scene, where Elizabeth leaves, I was ready for that final line, spoken into the total stillness of the auditorium: "In her letter to me Ba writes that she has taken Flush with her." I flung it out much more contemptuously than I ever had before. Take that, you swine! Everyone froze; then the curtain came down.

Maybe there's another high like that feeling right after a performance has ended, when you know it's gone well, but if so, I've never experienced it. Everyone looked euphoric. We all held hands tightly and came out for a joint curtain call, then one by one. The applause was loud and enthusiastic especially from some of the younger kids. It was while I was doing my solo curtain call that I saw Mom. She was sitting by herself, way off to one side, in her red dress. Our eyes met, and then I turned, smiled, curtsied, and swooped off the stage. Just as I did, a younger girl came up and handed me a bouquet of flowers and a single white rose. I looked at the notes attached to them while Vladimir was taking his bow. The flowers were from Daddy, the rose from Peter. I don't think of Peter as being that romantic. A single white rose seemed a wonderful present.

The curtain had come down. Mel, passing by me, suddenly reached over, grabbed me, and kissed me on the lips. "I've been wanting to do that for two months," he said.

A moment later, as I was standing there, slightly dazed, Brandemour came up to me. "Splendid, dear. You shot that last line out like a bolt of lightning. It made ripples go down my spine." She lowered her voice. "Leslie, I just had to tell you. I overheard some of the boys talking backstage, and one of them said, of you, 'If only she could be like that *off*stage!' "

I laughed.

Brandemour grabbed my arm. "Do it, Leslie! Let it all

out! You have a whole life ahead of you. Don't keep it in, for the sake of propriety or whatever. Do it!"

"Okay," I agreed happily, not sure exactly what I was agreeing to. I felt radiant, beautiful, talented, and possibly immortal. For the cast party I left on a lot of the makeup and even my hairpiece. The dressing room backstage is huge—we all share it. Peter came in with Daddy and Peter's mother and Muriel.

"Wonderful," Daddy said, hugging me. "I was so proud."

"Me too," said Peter's mother. "I was proud as the dickens."

"You can't be proud," Daddy said jocularly. "She's *my* daughter."

"Well, for tonight she's mine too," Peter's mother said. She bent down and whispered in my ear, "But I think you'd have been super as Elizabeth too."

I laughed. Everything seemed so funny and wonderful. I didn't care at all about not having been Elizabeth. I looked up at Peter. "Thanks for the rose," I said.

Peter was looking awkward, as though he wished he were somewhere else. "Well . . ." he murmured.

"Who was that large girl who played Elizabeth Barrett?" Muriel asked. "She was very impressive, didn't you think, Preston?"

"When Leslie was on stage, you couldn't look at anyone else," Daddy said. "She was the star."

"I thought the boy who played the father was the best," Peter said suddenly. Why does he do that, give me a rose and then say something to cut me down?

"He was excellent," Muriel said. "I couldn't believe it was a student production. Your director must be a very gifted woman."

"She likes to cast people against type," I explained. "Like, I wanted to be Elizabeth because I thought I was so much like her, but she thought playing Henrietta would be good for me."

"You're like both of them," Daddy said. "It's the two sides of your character."

Mel broke into our circle. "The party'll be at Vladimir's, Les. If you need a ride, we're leaving in fifteen minutes."

"Great," I called. I felt Peter hovering, scowling in the background. I hated him for spoiling the mood. "I guess I'll be back late," I told Daddy.

"Of course, of course," Daddy said. "I won't expect you back one minute before the crack of dawn."

"Oh, not *that* late!" I said, laughing.

"Not a minute before," he repeated. "You deserve a night of revelry to savor your triumph."

"I think we ought to leave and let Leslie get ready for the party," Peter's mother said. She bent down and kissed me. "Congratulations again."

I wondered if Mom would come backstage. I wanted her to.

Daddy hugged me. Peter just stood a few feet off, clearing his throat. "So—see you sometime," he said ironically. They all left.

What is wrong with him? I have this one fucking night when I do well, when I feel good, and he pulls that woebegone, forlorn thing, as though I were doing something bad! I couldn't have invited him to the cast party because you're not allowed to bring anyone who wasn't in the play or connected with it, not even other kids from the class. But even the way Peter had acted didn't destroy my mood. It was like there was still some drug going through me which made me feel anything was possible, I could be any way I wanted, any kind of person.

I looked up and saw Mom. "Hi, Les. I thought I'd wait till everyone had cleared out. You were terrific."

That meant a lot to me. "I wasn't sure if you were coming," I said, looking at her in the mirror.

"Yes, I wanted to." She looked pretty, but tired and ill at ease. Her right hand clutched at a small evening purse.

"Did Nelson come?" I wasn't sure if I should ask that.

"No." She smiled tightly. "He wasn't able to . . . to get away." She hesitated a moment, then said, "Well, I guess you must have a cast party. I just wanted to stop in."

"Thanks, Mom," I said, taking off my stage dress and getting out the flowered cotton dress I was wearing to the party.

She kissed me lightly on the cheek and disappeared. I didn't have time to think about it, but I was glad she had come, glad she'd thought I was good. I've never had an easy rapport with Mom, but perhaps because of that I feel glad when we achieve it even halfway.

I had a good time at the cast party. Even though I'd changed out of Henrietta's dress, I still felt, in some vague way, that I was Henrietta, that I could do things I wouldn't normally because they were the kinds of things she would have done and gotten away with. I sat on Vladimir's lap and drank the punch his mother had made. "What's *in* this?" I said. I still find him sexy, even if he is basically a jerk.

"Lab alcohol," he said. "My mother works at Einstein."

"Oh, that's where my . . . stepbrother works," I said.

"Is he the one I met?"

I nodded.

Bryna passed by and gave us a mock smile. "Two-timing me already, Robert!" she said sternly. "I haven't even written those sonnets yet! Think of world lit, kid!"

"Brandy said they weren't any good," Vladimir said.

"How do I love thee," I declaimed. "Let me count the ways. . . ."

Vladimir lifted me up. "Sorry, Les, you're getting heavy. Try the other knee."

"I think I'll get some more punch." I walked over to the table where they had some crackers and cheese.

Petra said, "Listen, thanks for covering for me in the first act. I was petrified."

"No one noticed," I said.

She looked at me intently. "You really look beautiful, Leslie. I mean it. You belong in the nineteenth century."

Maybe because Petra is gay, I'm never sure how to take remarks like that from her. "Thanks. I don't think I have a choice."

We danced some toward the end. Vladimir's father wouldn't let him use the stereo, but we got some good music on the radio. I danced with Vladimir, and Mel, and at the end Mira and I horsed around together. "I should've been in the play," she moaned. "I'm a jerk."

"But you wanted to learn how to do the lighting," I reminded her.

"That's all behind the scenes. I want to be up there—lights, applause! I felt so jealous of all of you!"

"You would have been good," I agreed.

"You should have been Elizabeth, and I could have been Henrietta," she said. "That would have been perfect."

My hairpiece fell down. Mel caught it and threw it across the room. "Leslie's going to pieces," he said. "Look, it's not real. What can you expect of these Windsor girls? Anything to hook a guy."

"Give it back!" I wailed. "It's not mine. I borrowed it."

I got it away from Vladimir, who pressed up against me insinuatingly. "What else isn't real, Les? Show us."

"Everything else is real," I said, looking him right in the eye. "But you're not the one who's going to see it, so bug off."

He assumed an expression of mock dismay. "Oh, so who's the lucky guy? Is *someone* going to? When? Where?"

"He's drunk," Mira whispered, taking my hand. "Don't bother with him."

I'd thought Mira would come home with me, but she said

she had to go shopping with her mother in the morning. I ended up taking a cab, letting Petra off at her apartment, which isn't far from Daddy's. It wasn't quite dawn when I got there, but almost, about four. I let myself in quietly.

Suddenly I felt like a balloon with all its helium leaking out, slowly but inexorably. Everything seemed sad and flat, and I knew I'd never be like Henrietta. That moment of feeling free and happy seemed like some weird illusion. It hadn't even lasted twelve hours! I sat in the living room, looking out into Gramercy Park, watching the sky lighten. At five twenty the phone rang.

"Hi," Peter said. "This is your wake-up call. It's the crack of dawn."

"Yes," I said wearily.

"Did it crack yet?"

"Probably."

There was a pause. "How was the cast party? Did you have fun?"

"Lots of fun," I said defiantly.

"I went right to sleep," Peter said, "but I set my alarm for five so I could say good night to you. You were great, Les."

"Thanks."

"I wish I were there now. I thought of coming over, but I didn't want your father losing his cool."

"Peter, I'm really tired. Let's talk in the morning."

"Dream of success," he said. "Dream of me."

I was too sleepy to figure out the conversation, but happy he'd called. Dream of success? Of him? Were they the same? Or opposed? But I didn't, as far as I know, dream of anything. I just fell into a deep, heavy sleep, glad to be in bed, safe, myself.

Moving Out

DAD MOVED OUT. HE NEVER SPOKE TO ME ABOUT IT. ONE day I came back from the lab, and there was a note on my pillow:

> Dear Peter,
>
> I'm moving to the Harvard Club. If you want to reach me, here's the number. Things have been difficult with Aline, what with various stresses and strains. I won't trouble you with the details. Hopefully we will work things out. Be good.
>
> Dad

It seemed absolutely ironic—here I wasn't "allowed" to stay with Leslie and her father, but I was stuck alone with her mother, whom I hardly know. In a way I felt like I was living alone. When I came back from the lab, no one was ever home. In the morning Aline left before I did.

Otherwise, when we ran into each other, she never referred to Dad's not being there. It was a little eerie, just the two of us in that huge, palatial apartment.

And then, two weeks before Leslie's graduation, Uncle Morgan died.

Mom called to tell me about it. I felt guilty, not having called him since the summer. Even though he was Dad's brother, I always thought of him in connection with Mom since she was the one who used to call him up and have him come for weekends sometimes.

"I feel so terrible," Mom said on the phone. "I don't know why it's hit me so hard. I knew he was sick. You just always think there'll be some miracle."

"Is there going to be a service?" I asked.

"I'll fly in tomorrow. I'll be staying at the Algonquin. . . . Could I speak to Nelson a sec?"

"He's not here," I said.

"What do you mean?"

"He moved out. He's staying at the Harvard Club."

There was a silence. "Why did he move out?" Mom wanted to know.

"I don't know."

"Well, I'll leave a message for him there. And I'll contact you tomorrow."

After Mom's call I saw Aline coming into the kitchen. She was in jeans and a white shirt. "My uncle just died," I said. "Dad's brother, Morgan. I guess I'll be going to the funeral tomorrow."

"Does Nelson know?"

"Mom's going to leave him a message."

"I assume he'll attend," she said, "if he doesn't have any more pressing engagement." She looked at me intently. "Has he been in touch with you, Peter, since he moved out?"

I shook my head.

"What kind of a person *is* he? He just leaves, not a word to his own child! How can he *be* so irresponsible?"

I shrugged. I really felt uncomfortable. "That's his personality, I guess."

"I hope you're not going to be like that when you grow up," she said, her eyes blazing.

"I don't think so."

"Everything comes too easily to him. He's spoiled, a spoiled child. I'm sorry to say that, but it's true."

"Yeah, I know," I said.

"I think you and your brothers have had a hard row to hoe with a role model like him," she said. "It could be really destructive. . . . Are you going to the funeral?"

I'd already told her I was, but I repeated that.

"Not that Nelson really gave a damn about Morgan either," she said, "but I'd think he would have the decency to appear. Who knows?"

Leslie and her father came to the service too. It was held in a small church downtown. There was no official religious service. Instead various friends of Morgan's got up and spoke about him, how they felt about him, what he'd meant to them. Mom really went to pieces. She started crying and couldn't stop, even when all the speeches were over. She held my hand tight. "I feel so terrible, Peter. It's such a loss."

Dad was there, looking solemn. He came over to us and patted Mom on the shoulder. "I'm sorry, Hope," he said, which was an odd remark since Morgan was his brother.

"I feel like I've lost a brother," Mom said. "More than a brother. He was such a kind, gentle person."

Leslie and her father had left right after the ceremony. "Where did Leslie go?" Mom said. "I didn't have a chance to talk to her or Preston."

"I guess they went home," I said.

"Isn't Leslie's home with you?" She looked from Dad to me.

Dad said, "Leslie's living with her father. We thought that would be best."

I walked Mom back to her hotel. "You mean he did this for one year?" she exclaimed. "One absurd *year* in which everyone's lives were shattered to pieces? One year?"

"Maybe they're not in love anymore," I offered. I didn't have a clue about Dad's motives for anything and never had.

"I feel sorry for Aline," Mom said. "I never thought I'd be saying this, but I do. She gave up a perfectly decent marriage, a fine husband . . . for what? She should've had a fling on the side and gotten him out of her system."

"But then you'd still be married to him," I pointed out.

"True," Mom said. She laughed bitterly. "And now I have a new life." Her eyes were all red, and she'd put her sunglasses on. "But I miss the old one, false and dopey as it was. I'm ashamed to say that, but I do."

Maybe if this had happened six months ago, I would have started hoping Mom and Dad would get back together. But now I didn't feel like there'd be any point to it. I thought of a fantasy Leslie had told me she'd had that Mom and her father would marry, the two left-overs, clinging to each other for comfort.

"Have you ever thought about Leslie's father?" I asked.

Mom looked distracted. "What about him?"

"I used to wish the two of your would get together."

Mom laughed. "Me and Preston? What an idea!"

"Don't you think he's a nice person?"

"Of course, I think he's a nice person, but what does that have to do with marrying anyone? Peter, I know you're very young still, but marriage has to be based on passion, on something inexplicable and mysterious, not just two people looking up and saying, 'Do you think it will rain today?' That's a travesty!"

I've rarely seen Mom so emotional. Maybe it was the funeral or hearing about Dad and Aline splitting up. But I also resented her saying "I know you're very young still."

"I'm eighteen," I said. "That's not so young."

"I didn't mean it in a derogatory way, sweetie. I just meant you haven't . . . I mean, as far as I know, your relations with girls haven't been that intense. Intellectually I've always felt you were very mature, much more so than Ken or Cliff."

I guess Mom really hadn't seen anything that time in Chicago. "I have a girl friend," I said. "I've had one all year."

She looked mildly surprised. "Have you? I'm so pleased. I was afraid once you moved to the city, you might lose touch with the girls in your class."

"Actually we're in love with each other," I said. "It's pretty serious."

Mom just beamed at me in her motherly way. "I'm so glad, Peter. Is she nice? Of course she must be if you like her."

"Yeah, she's terrific," I said. I felt buoyant and excited, even though I knew that we were talking about different things. I had the feeling Mom assumed the hypothetical girl and I weren't sleeping together, that we were just dating—having a romance.

Mom squeezed my hand. "She's very lucky, Peter. I hope she's aware of that. Some of these girls today are so calculating and heartless!" She peered at me in a concerneed way.

"Don't worry, Mom," I said. "I can handle it."

When we arrived at the hotel, Mom had to go up and get ready to fly back to Chicago. "It's going to take me a long time to get over this," she said as we parted. "I really loved Morgan. I felt he was Nelson's better half, what he might have been if only . . ."

She never finished the sentence.

* * *

I've been thinking about all the changes this year has made in my life: the divorce, living with Dad and Aline, Mom moving away, my affair with Leslie, Morgan's death. For seventeen years everything seemed very fixed and unmoving. My brothers went away to college, but that was about it. I've had friends who've lived in a dozen different states, gone to lots of different schools, even spent time in other countries. Whereas we always lived in the same house, I went to the same summer camp, the same school. Then one day I came home, and there'd been an earthquake, everything tossed high in the air, scattered to the four winds. Maybe I've been clinging to Leslie because she's part of my past, my childhood, and I don't want to feel everything is different. I suppose I imagined that it would all stay the same, and I would be the one to leave, go off to college, but now what's there to leave? My one big potential moment never happened. I never even really graduated formally. Mom's in Chicago; Dad's at the Harvard Club, and I'm alone in a ten-room apartment with Leslie's mother.

My work at the lab has gone pretty well. There were weeks when I worked doubly hard just because, with its tedious routine, it seemed the one still point in the turning world. But in the last couple of weeks I've been too disoriented to really concentrate. Even when I've been there, my mind has been elsewhere.

A few days after Uncle Morgan's funeral Rex Rosenblum called me into his office. I hadn't seen a whole lot of him. He was always rushing off to meetings or closeted in his office with this assistant or that.

"These are nice results," he said, looking over the work I'd left for him. "Very nice. . . . I gather it's been a hard year for you, Peter. I appreciate your taking this seriously."

"Hard in what way?" I said, not sure how much he knew about my family.

"Your father tells me his new marriage is on the skids and that he's already got a new 'friend' to keep his toes warm. God, the man's in his forties. I've known him for thirty years, and I don't think he's spent one *second* of his life without a woman! I'm envious as hell."

"I guess he likes them," I said.

"And they like him, that's what makes the difference. *I* like them too, but what do I have to show for it? One wife, no girl friends, no outside interests. Pretty pathetic, huh?"

I suspect I'll be like that, so I wouldn't be too quick to call it pathetic. I wonder who Dad's new girl friend is. He never said anything to me about anyone. In a way I'm sort of shocked, which may be childish. I thought he and Aline just weren't getting along. "What's her name?" I asked.

"What?"

'My father's new girl friend. I haven't met her yet."

He wrinkled up his nose. "Maybe I wasn't suppose to spill the beans. I thought you . . . Look, who knows if its even serious. If Nelson married all the dames he fools around with, he'd set some kind of world record. But she's cute, bright. The guy has good taste, damn him."

For the rest of the day I felt really angry. I don't want to hate my father, but there are times I feel like he doesn't give me much choice. He lets his former college roommate meet this woman, and for me, for his son, he just leaves a note saying, "I'm at the Harvard Club." Is *she* at the Harvard Club too?

The next morning I got a message that my father had called and left a studio number. I called him back from the phone booth in the lobby of the lab building. "Oh, hi, Pete," Dad said. "How's it going?"

"I got a message you'd called."

"Right . . . Well, I thought maybe now that . . . well, why don't the two of us have dinner? There's someone I'd like very much for you to meet."

"Who is it?" I sais warily.

"A very lovely person. She's wanted to meet you for a long time. I think you'll like each other a lot."

"Is this my next stepmother?" I said sarcastically. "Or just someone you're fucking?"

There was a pause. "We're meeting at Le Perigord at seven," Dad said in a chilly voice. "If you'd care to join us, we'd be delighted." He gave me the address.

I don't know what I want from Dad. Part of me wants to be his buddy, his friend, someone I feel he likes and respects. And part of me would like to see him screaming in some kind of agonizing pain, blubbering, apologetic. I remember when our class went to see *Death of a Salesman* last year, I almost envied the son because his father was such a pathetic failure, such a jerk. It seemed like that would be a lot easier than having a father who's successful at work, who women fall for, who leaves weeping wives in ten-room apartments without a thought.

But at the last minute I decided I did want to see my next potential stepmother. When I got to the restaurant, she was already at the table. Dad hadn't arrived yet. Her name was Monica Cartwright. She was a tall brunette, really pretty, at least fifteen years younger than my father. "I've been looking forward to this so much, Peter," she said, smiling.

I wish I'd come late. I didn't feel like sitting there trying to make small talk with her till Dad showed up. But she made it easy. She talked a lot, about herself, her work, her family. I just had to nod and mutter a few words from time to time. "So, are you going to marry him?" I said. I'd ordered a glass of wine, which I'd nervously drunk in about five minutes.

"I don't know if Nelson is the marrying kind," Monica said, laughing.

"He's done it twice."

"We may not be that compatible," she went on, brushing

back her hair. "I adore him, but my life is quite full and happy as it is. Marriage is way down the pike. For now I'm just glad to be there for him after this awful, traumatic year."

"What was so bad about it?" I meant what was so terrible for Dad? He seemed like the only person who hadn't suffered much.

Monica was on her second glass of wine. She had bright blue eyes with eye shadow around them. "Well, I gather he was tremendously devoted to your mother, even though they'd had so many problems. I doubt he would have even thought of divorce if Aline, if your stepmother, hadn't insisted. She sounds like a rather tyrannical person."

"Bullshit," I said. "He just does whatever he feels like. He felt like leaving Mom, so he left her. He wanted to marry Aline, so he married her. He never does anything he doesn't feel like doing."

Monica looked taken aback. "Nelson's such a generous, warm person. I hope you realize that, how much he cares for you *and* your brothers."

By the time Dad showed, half an hour late, I'd had two glasses of wine and was beginning to feel queasy. "Apologies all around," he said, kissing Monica. "The usual. What can I say. Peter, don't be an actor. Promise me that."

I said, in a slightly slurred voice, "Don't worry about it."

Once Dad was there, I shut up. I ordered a full dinner with black bean soup, steak medium rare with green peppercorns, which is my favorite dish, and asparagus on the side. I concentrated on eating.

"My son is very fond of food," Dad said dryly as I reached for a roll. "You'll have to excuse him."

I just looked at him.

"That looks delicious," Monica said. "Can I try a bite?" She reached over and speared some steak off my plate.

For dessert we had coffee, peach melba, and brandy. "Well, here's to the future," Dad said, raising his glass. "May it outdo the past!"

"To Peter and Harvard," Monica said.

"Monica went to Harvard," Dad put it. "She's as smart as she is beautiful."

"I hear you're a good lay too," I said and burped.

Dad turned red. "Peter, will you please apologize at once? That's *totally* uncalled for."

"Fuck off, Dad, will you?" I said. I got up and left the restaurant. When I was outside, I really felt sick. I'd had too much to eat and too much to drink. I also felt like a stupid jerk who'd acted like a baby.

I went back to the apartment and spent an hour throwing up. When I was done, I staggered into my room and lay there feeling like death. The phone rang. It was Leslie. I hadn't seen her since Uncle Morgan's funeral.

"You sound funny," she said. "Are you okay, Peter?"

"Les, I'm dying," I moaned. "I mean it." I started to cry. "Oh, Christ, everything's so stupid. I'm such a jerk."

"I love you," she said. "I'm coming over to get you."

Have a Good Life

I NEVER DID FIND OUT FROM PETER WHY HE WAS IN SUCH BAD shape that night when I went to Mom and Nelson's apartment. He was lying there on his bed like a beached whale, a wet washcloth over his face. "I can't move," he moaned. "I'm sick as a dog."

"What's wrong?" He seemed less hysterical than he'd been on the phone. I'd really gotten frightened at the way he sounded.

"I ate too much, I drank too much. I hate my father . . . he hates *me*."

I took the cloth off his face. "Should I make this cold again? How's your headache?"

Peter grabbed my hand and kissed it. "I love you," he said. "I want us to be together till we're ninety."

"We will," I said, laughing at his sudden change of mood.

"But you're going to Chicago, and I'll be at Harvard. What if you meet other guys?"

"What if you meet other girls?"

Peter half sat up. "I will *shun* other girls," he said solemnly. "I will be celibate. I won't even see movies with women. I'll lead a monastic, pure, scholarly existence." He burped.

"Lie down and shut up, okay?" I went to the bathroom, rinsed the washcloth in cold water, and came back.

"Maybe I'll be a monk," Peter said. "I'll be one of those guys who wears a saffron robe and waves tambourines in the air. I'll eschew all pleasures of the flesh."

I placed the washcloth over his forehead again. "How about me?" I said.

"We'll write each other," Peter said, closing his eyes. "We'll be like Abelard and Heloise."

"You mean you're going to be castrated? Yuck."

Peter reached up and took my hand. "Lie down next to me, okay?"

"What if Mom comes home?"

"She's never home."

"Where is she?"

"Dunno."

I lay down next to Peter. I felt wary. It was the first time I'd been back in the apartment since I'd moved out. "Maybe she and your father will get back together."

"Don't count on it."

"I'm not," I said. I rested my head on his shoulder, "I'm graduating next week."

"I can hardly wait," said Peter.

We talked for a while longer about various plans. As it evolved we decided to spend the summer driving to California and seeing the country. En route we would stop in Chicago and leave my stuff at Ken's girl friend's house till August, when I'd return and move into the dorm. It was great to think of that: two months of parentless freedom, traveling, talking, making love, whatever we felt like.

It was all I could do to get through exam week. Everything at Windsor seemed like a letdown after the play. Classes were dull—and most of us had cut them anyway. Even the teachers seemed spaced out and forgetful, like they were looking ahead to summer vacation.

"I hope you'll come back and see me," Brandemour had said when I went in to say good-bye to her.

"I will," I promised.

"Will you keep on with your acting? I hope so much you do."

"If I think I'm talented enough to make it," I said. "But I'm not sure."

"Talent is the tip of the iceberg," Brandemour said, lighting a cigarillo. "It's tenacity that counts. You have to have a quart of tenacity for every teaspoonful of talent. I think you do, Leslie. There's a lot under the surface still. Draw on it. *Use* it."

"Okay," I said lightly. "I'll try."

"I'm sure it's presumptuous of me even to raise such an issue, but don't marry till you're thirty or thirty-five. Give yourself years to expand, to grow, to experiment. I hate seeing my girls return all sewn up into these ghastly little marriages to lawyers and doctors. They haven't even tried! Give it *everything*! What do you have to lose?"

"Have you ever been married?" I asked. There were so many rumors about Brandy, that she was gay, that she was from a wealthy family who'd disowned her because she'd made an improper marriage.

"I married at nineteen," Brandemour said, rolling her eyes. "A banker from Philadelphia, can you believe it? I think he married me just to cause his mother to have a heart attack, which she did, and of course I've always had that insane, irrepressible attraction to stuffy men that plagues so many bohemian girls. What I'm saying is do as I say, not as I did."

"And was that it?" I pursued. "Did you ever meet anyone again who—"

She laughed. "Countless people, each one more inappropriate than the last. My life has been an endless series of personal disasters too absurd and unlikely even to provide material for a surrealist comedy. But why all the questions? Are you in love, dear?"

"I think so. I'm not sure."

She crushed out her cigarillo. "Don't get me wrong. I'm not against passion. Passion is grand and glorious, and don't ever let anyone tell you otherwise. Just don't nail yourself in. Use men, in the best sense, to explore, to have pleasure, to enjoy. They use us. We have to learn to use them."

"I'll try to remember all that," I said.

Brandemour smiled at me fondly. "Sometimes when I look at you, Leslie, I see myself, transported back so many years, and I feel a terrible pang. Maybe it's because I never had children." She leaned over and kissed me. "Have a good life, and come back and tell me all about it."

I said good-bye to some of the other teachers, but it was only what Brandemour said that stuck with me. I knew I'd remember it, whether it proved helpful or not. And already, before graduation even, I had fantasies of returning to school, having just gotten the lead in a Broadway play, telling her about it.

On the last day of exams Mira and I went to Riverside Park. Her mother's boyfriend had gotten her a job in France as an au pair for a French family in Nice. Mira is really fluent in French; her accent is perfect.

"Should I look up Jacques?" she asked. We were sitting under a tree, staring out at the river. "Do you think he'll remember me?"

"Sure," I said easily, just wanting to say whatever she wanted to hear. "You always remember first love."

Mira made a face. "It was first for me, more like twentieth for him. French guys start early. Still, I think I was his first American. I'm thinking of cutting all my hair off—what do you think?"

I was horrified. Mira's long frizzy blond hair is so beautiful, it's like her trademark. "Why?"

"I want a new image, more breezy. Will you come with me while I have it done? Hold my hand?"

"Sure."

I hadn't known she meant it literally, but the next day she dragged me to a beauty parlor, and I had to sit right beside her, holding her hand, or rather, letting her clutch mine. Her eyes looked big and terrified as her soft honey-colored hair cascaded down to the floor. When it was done, it was chin length, a thick bob, swinging back and forth. "You still look beautiful," I said. I'd been half-hoping she wouldn't.

"Yeah, I do," Mira said, regarding herself philosophically. She crawled around on the floor and stuffed all the hair into a paper shopping bag. "Poor Jacques, he'll take one look at me and fall into a faint, thereby breaking the heart of his poor French sweetheart."

"Or wife." I couldn't resist pointing out that possiblity.

"I doubt it. He said he wouldn't marry till he was thirty-five."

The week after graduation Peter came over every day. Daddy was at work, Peter had stopped going to the lab, and I was free for the summer. The weather had suddenly turned hot and we spent our time playing handball, loafing around in our underwear, and making love.

Probably I should have worried that Daddy would come home early some afternoon and find us making love on the living room floor, but I knew he wouldn't, and he didn't. Our luck had held out this far. I knew it would continue.

One morning Peter took me to a new place to play handball, and I beat him, of course.

"Jesus, you're merciless," he said, sweating, his face a brilliant pink. "How do I stand it?"

"I *love* beating men at sports!" I said. "It's the greatest high."

"But I'm a mere boy, a helpless, gentle, feminist boy."

"Bullshit."

Peter rolled his eyes back in his head. "These sex-crazed modern females," he gasped. "They beat men at handball, suck their vital juices, leave us limp, inert. . . ."

I kissed him. "Let's go back to the apartment. I want to give you something to think about when you're in a monastery."

With all the fun of horsing around, I forgot that I couldn't just take off with Peter for California. For one thing I had to go back to Mom and Nelson's apartment to get all my stuff. I have a trunk, and I knew all my clothes would fit into it, but there were books, a few stuffed animals, and some paintings too. Peter promised to come and help me.

I knew I should see Mom before I left, knew she was waiting for me to make a move toward her since she'd made the move of coming to the play and going backstage to congratulate me. Stealing off like a thief in the night would be stupid. We'd broken the news that we were leaving to Daddy and I assumed he'd told Mom, but I hadn't wanted to ask Daddy what her reaction was. I knew I should talk to her before I left—but what could I say? Was I really sorry I'd moved out? No. I was sorry for the way I'd done it, so suddenly, sorry we hadn't talked more about what was happening. I wonder if I could have gone to her and told her about Peter. If she'd known about our relationship, she would've understood more of what I was going through.

Peter and I went to the apartment on a hot, overcast afternoon. Mom wasn't there, and the place had a strange vacant look, even though all the furniture was still there. Maybe it was that everything was so new. Mom had taken almost nothing from our old apartment. "It looks like a mausoleum," I said.

My room was horribly stuffy. The windows were closed. I flipped on the air-conditioner and started throwing things from my bureau into the trunk. Peter just sat and watched. He'd come more for moral support than anything else. At one point he jumped up and left the room and came back with four of my Dior bikini underpants. "I believe these are yours," he said.

"God, where were they? I've been looking for them everywhere."

He looked sheepish. "I've been sleeping with them."

"Peter!"

"I stole them last summer. They played an active role in my fantasy life earlier this year. While you were acting so hardhearted and distant, I at least had these."

Maybe this is some basic distinction between the sexes. I can't imagine getting a sexual charge out of sleeping with Peter's jockey shorts. Peter began holding each of the bikinis up in turn. "This one I call Gloria. And this is Sophie. The pink one is Eleanor."

I snatched them away from him. "You are perverse. Will you at least help me?"

He bowed. "At your service. What does madam require?"

I looked around the room. The bureau was empty, and I'd packed most of the books. "I think I need three or four more boxes. Could you go to the liquor store or the supermarket and see if they can spare a few?"

After Peter left, I lay down on the bed. By now the room was cool. I felt wiped out. I dozed off briefly and woke up when I heard the door opening. I looked up, expecting Peter. It was Mom.

"Leslie!" She looked shocked.

Suddenly I felt guilty at the thought that I'd have just left like that, without saying good-bye. "I'm shipping some of my stuff to Chicago," I said. "Ken said I could store it in their basement till I get a place to stay."

Despite the heat Mom looked cool and lovely in a pale-blue dress and white sandals. "Until your father told me about this cross-country trip, I hadn't realized you and Peter were such good friends."

"We see each other sometimes," I said awkwardly, picking at a thread on the bed.

Mom looked at the Matisse poster on the wall.

"What—what's happening?" I stammered.

"About what?"

"Are you and Nelson getting back together?"

She shook her head. "No. I had to face it—it's over. I feel like a fool, having thought I could make Nelson commit himself to one woman. He never will. But you know, it wasn't working with Daddy. Maybe I have to be grateful to Nelson for that, giving me a push—"

"Toward what?"

"It's time I found out what *not* being married is like. I've put in twenty-four years back to back. I think celibacy might almost be peaceful."

I can't imagine Mom alone. Whenever I think of her, it's with a man, laughing, flirting. "It sounds good," I said.

"I've set you a terrible example," she said. "I've gone around saying how independent I am, but what has it boiled down to?"

"Your work," I said. "You're financially independent. They say that comes first."

"Maybe." She looked thoughtful. "Are you happy now, Leslie?"

"I—yes." I wasn't sure how she meant that.

"I wish I'd had the courage to just leave Preston. I wish you and I could've had this year together. Instead all I thought about was Nelson, and the only effect that had was to drive him away. Not that he wouldn't have strayed eventually anyway, but I think I helped the process along."

I stood up. "I think we did get to know each other," I said. "And I'm not moving away permanently. I'll be back. We'll be in touch."

Mom held me. "I hope so. I'm going to miss you, hon."

Peter's body is round, but it's also soft and squeezable, huggable, comforting. Mom is so small and delicate, and I always feel we make physical contact in a gingerly way, as though there was a barrier between us. I wanted her to seal our conversation by saying "I love you," but she didn't.

A moment later Peter returned with the boxes. "I'm helping Leslie pack," he said, looking nervous.

"I'm glad you were able to get extra boxes," Mom said. "How about your stuff, Peter?"

"Right—well, I'll come around sometime next week. Is that okay?"

"I was under the impression you were still living here. Have you moved out?"

"I just meant I need to get all my stuff together," Peter said.

"Are you a good driver?" Mom said. "Cross country is a long trip." We'd already gone over all of that with Daddy. He'd been pretty reluctant at first to let me go.

"I'm excellent," Peter said. "Very careful."

"Well, I trust you," Mom said.

She left the room, and Peter and I packed the rest of the stuff quickly, not talking to each other.

Finally the day of our departure arrived. We'd already shipped the trunk and most of my belongings to Chicago and were just taking some boxes and two suitcases in the secondhand car Peter had bought with his graduation money.

Daddy hovered over us, watching us pack the car. "You'll drive extremely carefully," he said, "won't you, Peter?"

I think Peter is beginning to realize what it's like to be an only child. He used to think I was so lucky. "Daddy, he never goes over fifty. And we'll wear our seat belts all the time."

"*All* the time," Daddy repeated. "Even for the shortest distances. This may sound obsessive, but it's terribly important."

I hugged him. "I'll call you from Chicago."

"Call any time you want. Always make it collect." He looked so downcast I felt I might cry.

"I will." I got into the car and waved at him, feeling my throat tighten.

Peter drove the car down Central Park West. "Hey, are you crying?"

"Sort of—not really." I looked at him. "You know, I just realized something. We're not brother and sister anymore."

"Were we ever?"

"Legally we were—well, stepbrother and stepsister, anyway. What are we now?"

Peter put his hand on my shoulder. "Anything we want to be, Les."

About the Author

Norma Klein is the immensely popular author of novels for adults, young adults and children. Her books for Fawcett include ANGEL FACE, BEGINNERS' LOVE, IT'S OKAY IF YOU DON'T LOVE ME, LOVE IS ONE OF THE CHOICES, THE QUEEN OF WHAT IFS, BIZOU, SNAPSHOTS, GIVE AND TAKE and THE CHEERLEADER.

Ms. Klein grew up in New York City. She lives on the Upper West Side of Manhattan with her husband and two teenage daughters.